THE MUSEUM AT
PURGATORY

THE MUSEUM AT PURGATORY

NICK BANTOCK

A BYZANTIUM BOOK

HarperCollinsPublishers

*T*O THE ANARCHISTS, THE ANGELS, AND
EVERYONE WHO HAS EVER ENCOURAGED ME.

Printed in China.

LIBRARY OF CONGRESS CATALOGING-IN-PUBLICATION DATA:
Bantock, Nick.
  The museum at Purgatory / Nick Bantock. — 1st ed.
   p. cm.
  ISBN 0-06-757546-3
  I. Title.
 PR6052.A54M87   1999
 823'.914—dc21   98-53766
           CIP

Art Direction: Barbara Hodgson / Byzantium Books Inc.
Book design: Isabelle Swiderski / Byzantium Books Inc.
Composition: Byzantium Books Inc.

ACKNOWLEDGMENTS:
The photographs in this book were taken by PIXL of Burnaby, B.C.
Teresa Tiemstra, Troy Gray and Jesús Gonzalez did the lion's share of the work,
while Simon Fong and Rob Sischy ably assisted. I'd like to thank each of them
for a superb job.

Shrine carpentry by the remarkable Mr. Nick Hughes

Readers and advisors: Barbara Hodgson, Kim Kasasian, Alix Kitchen,
Joseph Montebello, Ed Nelson, Anja Schmidt, Dawna Stromsoe,
Isabelle Swiderski, and Iris Tupholme. Additional thanks to Liz Darhansoff
and Sara Allen, for her monstrous regiment.

CONTENTS

AN INTRODUCTION

PREVIOUS PAGE:

Crescent Mask,
Entrance Hall.

FACING PAGE:

Hurtago's Horn of the
Moon, Gazio Room.

I met Marie Louise Gornier the other day, she'd only been dead for a week or so. Considering the things I'd done to her while she was alive, she looked remarkably fit and healthy.

We sat in a Turkish cafe not far from the Museum and talked about our first encounter—the way I'd examined her, lured her with my promises and run my hands over her body. I found myself wanting to touch her again, just to feel her unblemished skin. She asked to hear my side of the story—why I'd abused her trust. What could I say? That I was obsessed with beauty? No, that would have been dismissive. So I told her what I knew of the motivation behind my actions. In fact, I did the best I could to explain my blackened heart. I watched for anger to appear on her face, but of course, given that we were in Purgatory, that wasn't likely. When I'd finished my explanation, she thanked me for my honesty and gathered herself to leave. I didn't want her to go. I needed more. Surely I wasn't planning a new seduction? Then it dawned on me; it was for-giveness that I longed for. How naive could I be? I stood, shook her hand, and watched her walk away. As she left, the cafe's plump

patterned cushions began to turn into Shaker chairs and the thick black coffee we'd been drinking thinned itself into Jamaican lemonade. I wondered which of us precipitated the alterations, but it was impossible to tell.

My name is Non, and as Curator of the Museum here at Purgatory I am required by statute to facilitate, without judgment, the progress of all collectors assigned to these halls. It is my responsibility to act as their souls' guardian, as well as preserver of their accumulated treasures. These objectives I adhere to, though I can't in all honesty say I'm utterly devoid of prejudice, nor do I think I'm the right person to be a soul's guardian. Nevertheless, I *am* the Curator, and I carry out my obligations to the best of my ability.

What you are about to see and read is a catalogue of objects and events. A catalogue not in the sense of an official museum directory, but a singular selection of people, their collections, and the extent to which they are a part of me. The first section is broken into ten chapters, one for each of the chosen rooms. I have included within these chapters a visual account of the collectors' artifacts, as well as a brief description of their experiences. However, before I proceed, it would probably be wise if I acquainted you with the Museum and, for that matter, the city itself. Purgatory is complex, so I ask you to bear with me if my initial description seems a little terse—later, when you

come to section two of this volume ("The Curator's Tale"), you will no doubt gain a more rounded picture of the city and its population.

Purgatory takes a meditative, non-partisan view of reality. This ambiguous position is possible thanks to its geographical placement, midway between the earthly community and the region presided over by the Utopian States (those provinces that lay emphasis on recuperation) and the Dystopian States (whose dictum forcibly discourages indulgence and foppery).

Prompted by the advent of death, visitors to Purgatory are faced with the fundamental questions of self-worth. Occasionally, resolution of these knotty problems can be hastily achieved, however inner turmoil often requires extended consideration in order to smooth out any imbalances. In the case of those *indecisives* (or ex-amnesiacs like me) who need a lengthier period to weigh their actions, Purgatory offers an environment conducive to the orchestration of clarity.

To understand the method of self-evaluation employed by Purgatory's visitors, one must first comprehend the basic premise of life. It would seem that we spend our waking days gathering information—our experiences, thoughts, and feelings all constitute a form of data. When we sleep we deposit these findings, transmitting the information via dream images into a well of collective consciousness. This Dreamwell (which is also death's portal into Purgatory) is a swelling biotic storehouse, constantly absorbing and filtering everything it receives. Amazing, is it not, that our egocentricities lead us into viewing dreams as either irrelevant surrealism or a private psycho-oracular message service, when in fact dreams are merely the back-projected discharges of our own sensory gatherings.

Not surprisingly, after being made aware of the above, new-comers to the city are prone to a variety of responses, ranging from exasperation to exalted relief. When I was informed of the reason for existence by my predecessor Curator Vey, my reaction was to burst into laughter, though to this day I'm not certain whether I considered it comedy or tragedy.

Assessing oneself after death is a matter of measuring the information acquired during life. What, we are obliged to ask ourselves, have we contributed to the greater consciousness? The answer to this far from easy question defines whether our next port of call is one of the Utopias or Dystopias.

In order to travel on from Purgatory, a spectral being must come to terms with those conflicting elements not dealt with previously. No godlike external judge is going to decide the being's destination—the Utopian or Dystopian State chosen must reflect the specific need of the spirit in question.

Purgatory's physical form can be confusing (it certainly was to me!). Its shape and configuration remain in constant flux, yet it has always existed in its present manifestation. Its structures are an edgeless mix of cultural and architectural styles that

FACING PAGE:

Pre-Minervan stave script, Sengler Room.

BELOW:

Asiatic Boxwood Equestrian, Winter Room.

interchange to accommodate era and race. Byzantine polygon-domed cathedrals become Nubian huts, Alexandrian gutter alleys turn into Hindu temples—the city is infinitely flexible.

The Museum itself is unique. Unlike the rest of the city's chameleonesque landscape the building's facade remains unchanged, but its interior unfolds limitlessly. By utilizing an architectural system of Mobius expansion, the infinite cubic capacity allows an unrestricted exhibition space within a structure of minimal exterior dimension.

As for the heirlooms housed here, they come from two distinct sources—collections (in part or whole) that have accompanied our guests as they passed through the Dreamwell into Purgatory, and works created by the city's inhabitants during their stay here. No works may travel beyond Purgatory, therefore all items, whether brought in or constructed during residence, stay inside these galleries for perpetuity.

While studying the words and images within this volume, the reader should be reminded that the Museum houses objects whose history is authentic but whose actuality fails to reside in the regular precepts of normality.

PART ONE
Catalogue of Galleries

THE WINTER ROOM

*A*lice Seline Winter's method of collecting had little to do with historical significance, rather it reflected her idiosyncratic perception of grace.

She told me that she'd begun acquiring her collection of collections on a small scale, purchasing individual pieces from flea markets and antique stores. Later, as the impetus grew, she migrated to auction houses, buying those lots listed as curious or odd. Her tastes were nonspecific. Having minimal interest in fashionable items like paintings or porcelain, she directed her attentions towards those objects that she was able to comfortably identify with.

By the time she died, she held a vast inventory of eccentrica under her roof. Brought together here, in the Winter Room, is a small but representative selection of her collections.

Her *Tobac Cards* and the *Gaelic Labels* were assembled from numerous smaller holdings, obtained over an extended period. The *Rockbone* collection includes various examples of proximity assimilation, a phenomenon occurring when minerals, plants and skeletal tissue combine through convergence.

Obscure Objects

Comparably, the *Mossbacked Taxidermy* collection is suffused with a musty arthritic pathos.

Winter understood that collecting could be a spiritually intuitive act and not just an acquisitive artform. Her talent lay in her ability to recognize connections, and was probably best represented by the gathering of *Sacred Bundles*. These assemblages originated in many different communities and had little in common apart from their bindings. Yet Winter sensed that within their disparateness a universality lingered.

Timid as a pigmy sparrow (more than once I resisted the compulsion to offer her bread crumbs), Winter spent most of her adult life alone, hiding behind the meaninglessness of her bean-quota job, and avoiding communication or contact with her insensitive and overly gregarious co-workers.

When Alice was a child her mother had berated her for her bent head, downcast eyes, and concave torso, telling her she was inconsequential, boring, and hopelessly ordinary. Winter came to believe the self-fulfilling truth in her mother's words, certain that the shallowness of her breathing and quietness of her heartbeat were worthy of mockery. The idea of being humiliated still further kept her buried deep within herself. After the death of her mother, she remained in the house where she'd grown up, outwardly staid, inwardly yearning for a liberation from shyness.

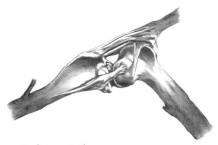

Early twentieth-century medical illustration of a mango ball and socket joint; two late nineteenth-century colored engravings of crystal-teeth formulations.
THE ROCKBONE COLLECTION

Articulated bobcat.
THE MOSSBACKED
TAXIDERMY

By the time Alice drew the winning ticket on the National Lottery, she was already a middle-aged, semi-reclusive dreamer. However, her reveries were far from mundane, revolving as they did around an imaginary museum of aberrational artifacts. She believed that the cure for her ordinariness was to acquire unique and unusual things. She felt convinced that somehow the power of these articles would rub off on her, and that, as if by osmosis, she'd feel confident and accepted.

Winter told no one of her sudden, massive fortune. She initially resisted the inclination to give notice and stayed at her place of employment, savoring her secret, watching the office go through its unchanging petty rituals, the staff oblivious to her transformation. (I understand her mode of passive revenge, though if it had been me I think I would have been tempted to burn down the premises or at least leave it awash in vichyssoise.)

However, Alice made her own plans, and as is the way with the advent of great wealth, was able to maneuver her fantasy towards a reality. After three months, she abandoned her job, her mother's house, and the town she'd been born in, crossed the country and installed herself in a coastal metropolis. There she bought a cavernous warehouse and converted it into a private museum, where she could roam amongst her chosen objects of obscurity.

Winter's museum-home grew, but instead of emerging into the world, she found herself retreating still further from it—burying herself into the seclusion of her sanctum, cleaning cabinets, organizing and reorganizing, purchasing ever more collections, and wallowing in the moanings of the harbor lighthouse foghorn.

Painted Pelonese parrot, from the Malvern collection of wooden birds.

When she came to Purgatory to study her life, she learned that compulsive collectors are inclined to exhibit an inability to form an overview. She had always had the innate belief that control and arrangement of small detail would compensate for her fear of encounter. Here, in the museum, she became obliged to admit that she'd evaded her life's potential. Her lack of commitment and dread of failure forced her to obstruct her soul's willingness to participate.

I pointed out that she had maintained a strong affinity with her collections, which were far from lacking in vitality, and undoubtedly she'd succeeded in overcoming a little of her petrified insulation. But she knew only too well that she had not made significant enough advances to progress to any of the Utopian or Dystopian States. Therefore her only recourse was to apply for a return. To be reborn in her previous confines, within the same time span and body, but with the consolation that a certain residual insight would make the next incarnation a little less lonely.

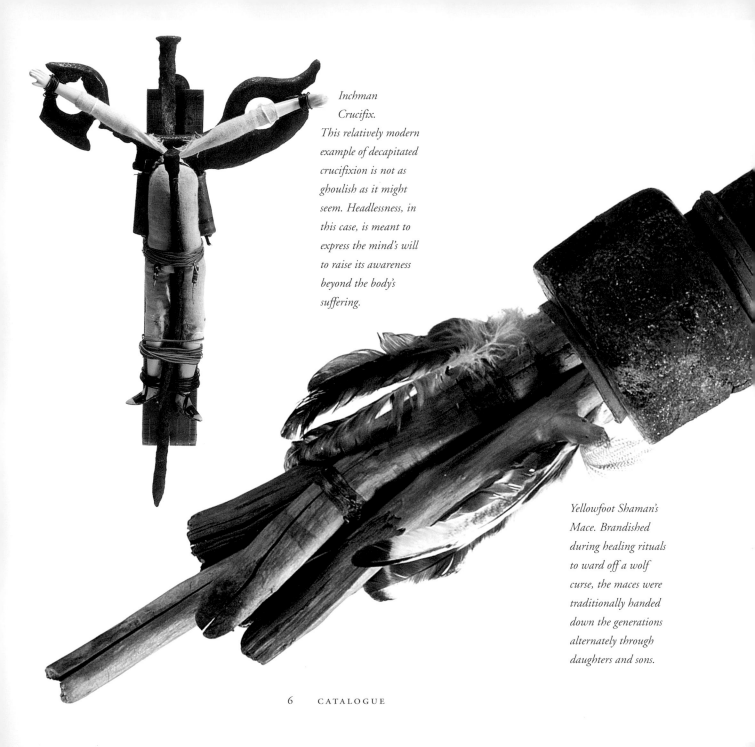

Inchman Crucifix. This relatively modern example of decapitated crucifixion is not as ghoulish as it might seem. Headlessness, in this case, is meant to express the mind's will to raise its awareness beyond the body's suffering.

Yellowfoot Shaman's Mace. Brandished during healing rituals to ward off a wolf curse, the maces were traditionally handed down the generations alternately through daughters and sons.

Sacred Bundles

ABOVE: *Shorewashed Rope Balls. Used as fertility emblems by the Tanakur people, the bundles (symbolizing entwined umbilical cords) were buried in sand for three cycles of the moon before being dug up, unwound, and strung out to receive the sun.*

LEFT: *I Ching Wall Hanging. The Upper section represents the four seasons, while the holes give channel through which the four winds may blow. The center symbol denotes house of ownership. The yarrow sticks are painted red and black to remind the Superior man that change is inevitable.*

The Rockbone
Collection

ABOVE: *Hogstusk
incarcerated in a
pit-barnacle castle.*

LEFT: *Buffalo
and coyote molars
assimilated by a
Rozen rock crystal.*

LEFT: *Blue razorshell*
surmounted by
barnacles and a
cumbertree.

FAR LEFT: *Impala*
mandible snared
by a cedarknot.

Tobac Cards

Beauties of all Nations
JAPANESE.

A. BAKER & Cº Ltd.

PLAYER'S CIGARETTES.

"LAZY-TONGS" FIRE-ESCAPE.

PLAYER'S CIGARETTES.

LINE-THROWING GUN IN USE.

PLAYER'S CIGARETTES.

AUTOMATIC SPRAYING HELMET IN USE.

PLAYER'S CIGARETTES.

"QUADRICYCLE" "FIRST-AID" HOSE-CARRIER, 1895.

WILLS'S CIGARETTES.

THREE-HANDED SEAT.

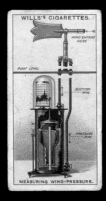

WILLS'S CIGARETTES.

MEASURING WIND-PRESSURE.

WILLS'S CIGARETTES

MENDING ELECTRIC WIRES

WILLS'S CIGARETTES.

X

U

PLAYER'S CIGARETTES

SPRINGBOK

WILLS'S CIGARETTES

AUGUST MANNS.

WILLS'S CIGARETTES.

PARACHUTE DESCENT BY GARNERIN, 1797.

Player's Cigarettes

Indian Ring-Necked Parrakeet

PLAYER'S CIGARETTES

BEWARE OF TRAM LINES

Gaelic Labels

CLOCKWISE
FROM TOP LEFT:
Snaptail Alligator,
Piped Cobra,
Pygmy Hedgehog,
Houlin Iguana,
Delinquent Puffer fish,
Surf Martin.

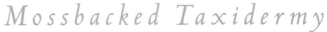

Mossbacked Taxidermy

Winter was attracted to the Mossbacked Taxidermy *because of its disheveled and anatomically idiosyncratic demeanor. She kept the badly stuffed animals uncleaned, feeling that the dust gave them an air of aging dignity.*

THE FITZGERALD ROOM

Edward Fitzgerald, who was best known for his translations of *The Rubaiyat of Omar Khayyam*, brought to the Museum a collection of six carpets imbued with magic.

(Contrary to popular myth, magic carpets do not fly, they are looked into, much the same way one looks at the images dancing within a fire. Flame images tend to be random, but a magic carpet's iris holds a series of sequential events locked within the warp and weft for as long as the threads survive. These contained pictures are not there at first sight; it takes skill, practice, and a cipher, to slide through the patterns and travel to the carpet's memory.)

Fitzgerald was the seventh of eight children born to a country gentleman, and he enjoyed all the privileges that a wealthy Victorian home could offer.

By the age of twenty-one he had already received his degree from Trinity College, Cambridge, and had moved to Paris, where he saw fit to expand his worldly experiences. He envisioned himself as a young scholar, dedicated to plain living and high thinking, and his minor indulgences were far from hedonistic

Magic Carpets

(common ground I can hardly claim to share). He attempted to maintain this self image throughout his life, shunning excessive materialism and focusing principally on translating literary works from Greek, Latin, Spanish, and Persian.

He was well confirmed in his middle-aged bachelordom, when he married Lucy Barton, the daughter of a recently deceased friend. The couple could not have been less suited, and the arrangement lasted a tortuous six months. At the marriage's demise Fitzgerald retreated to a safe distance, in an even more depressed condition than the one in which he had entered the union.

It was in that bruised mindframe that he stumbled into the year 1857, and his encounter with a young Persian woman.

In his letter of self-declaration (exhibited), Fitzgerald accurately describes his life's plight and his subsequent collapse into despondency. After his failure to find Khayyam's key, Fitzgerald turned towards his only solace—the sea. He died in stiff-lipped discontent, at the age of seventy-four.

Fitzgerald's Letter

Due to the poor legibility of Fitzgerald's handwriting the following has been transcribed into printed text.

While in Suffolk, I contrived to spend my days sailing with the fishermen of Lowestoft, and my nights studiously translating foreign texts. I was introspective and uncomfortable in myself, and my jaundiced view of the world was not enhanced by the events of eighteen fifty-seven.

Under iron-gray skies, on an afternoon in early April that year, I helped bring ashore the passengers and crew from a Dutch schooner that had gone down in a squall. Amidst the shivering, shocked survivors was a young Persian woman whose calm demeanor and striking features much impressed me.

The woman was given board at the vicarage, and in the days that followed I visited her on a number of occasions. As a linguist I had acquired an adequate command of Persian five years previously, and at the vicar's request helped the woman who called herself Basa make arrangements to continue her journey. To my unexpected pleasure, I found Basa highly educated and infinitely more companionable than Lucy, the woman I had disastrously married the previous year. During one of our conversations Basa began extolling the virtues of the eleventh-century Persian poet Omar Khayyam. I listened with great interest and said I would make a note to search out his work next time I was in Oxford. This, however, did not satisfy her and she urged me to write to the Bodleian library, requesting that they find the verses for me. It was clear that her motive went beyond my poetic education, and when I pressed her, she agreed to explain her insistence only if I promised to look after something that she intended to send me at a later date.

Intrigue aroused, I readily concurred, sensing that I was about to be taken into the confidence of this beguiling creature.

Basa then proceeded to recite a chronicle that contained much more than I bargained for—

"On a sweet scented summer evening, I was led by my husband, who I loved and trusted in all matters, to a secluded garden in the grounds of the Sultan's palace. When we came to a casement window, set within the wall, he tapped covertly on the shutters. After a few seconds they parted and we were confronted by a woman whose face was shielded behind a polished black mask. Her muffled, rasping voice informed me that I'd been selected to assist in an affair of state. I was handed an etched goblet, bound inside a cloth map, and instructed to follow the marked directions. She insisted that I must go immediately to a village north of Isfahan, where I was to deliver the goblet. The window closed abruptly, leaving me nervously clinging to my unexpected charge. My husband then accompanied me to the garden's edge, where he embraced me, assured me all was as it should be, and bade me farewell.

"The journey took many days. When I reached the village I was dirty and exhausted but I found the indicated house and handed over the cup. Without halting I turned and headed homeward. The moment I arrived back in the city I was seized by the Sultan's Guard, thrown into prison, and inquisitioned. But I was never tried, and after many months I was released from captivity. No reason for my incarceration was given. The authorities would only tell me that my name had been cleared and that the conspiracy against the Sultan had been dealt with. I returned home elated to have survived my ordeal, and eager to be reunited with my husband. But he was nowhere to be found—he had vanished without trace.

"I could not accept my loss, or the wrongs perpetrated against me. Yet I felt powerless. Finally, in desperation, I went to the bazaar to find the weaver of Seeing Carpets. I asked him to make me the means by which I might discover the whereabouts of my husband, and the reason for my incarceration. He agreed to weave a set of rugs but cautioned me that the highly curious carpets would henceforth indiscriminately watch the movements of anyone falling within the field of their vision.

"When the carpets were complete, the weaver carefully outlined with his finger the Khayyam cryptic he'd inserted into the design, saying that a section of verse had to be recited aloud, for the carpets to awaken.

"I had the six carpets carried to my home, and there I looked deep into their central patterns. I saw myself in the garden, and I saw my husband watch me depart, before retracing his steps to the window and the woman. When she lowered her mask I saw the terrible cruelty in her eyes, I heard her whisper in his ear, and laugh as she viciously pulled his head down to her breasts.

"I saw my journey, and my arrest. I saw my faithless husband dragged from his bed and I saw his cursory trial and beheading. And then I watched while his seductress slipped past the border guards to make her escape into Russia.

"I set out on a mission of revenge, pursuing my betrayer across half of Asia and most of Europe. I followed her to St. Petersburg where she poisoned a family for their gold, and to Constantinople where she slit the throat of a courtesan for an insult. I traced her trail of despotism and slowly closed in on her. I was on my way to Gothenburg, only hours behind her, when my ship was dragged off course and swallowed by the sea.

"Thus far she has eluded me, but I swear to you that before this year is through I will wash my hands in her blood."

I was horrified, fascinated; what could I say? I begged her to tell me more, but she refused, saying that she'd revealed too much already.

Over the next couple of days I saw her as often as good manners would permit. Rather than deter me, Basa's dark tale stimulated my heart and I was forced to admit to myself, if not her, that I was falling in love.

The evening before she was to travel on, I indulged in a little too much of the good parson's sherry, and found myself proposing to Basa. She teased me, and solemnly pointed out that I was already spoken for. I made jest of my indiscretion and disguised the true intensity of my feelings, hiding the fact that my marriage had already ended in separation. The evening continued in a light vein, and at ten, before my mood could turn to dejection, I kissed her hand and asked the vicar's servant for my coat and gloves. I bowed and headed for the door, but Basa followed me to the hallway, thanked me for my kindnesses and bade me once again to research the poems of Omar Khayyam, adding that they would be of as much importance to me as they were to her.

That autumn, there came from Sweden a wooden crate containing a very large elongated parcel. I unwrapped the paper and twine and discovered six magnificent Persian carpets. I hung them around my living room and examined them carefully. They had about them, a strangeness that was difficult to define. Even though they were unaccompanied by a note, there could be no question who they came from, and my longing for Basa welled up again with a renewed ferocity.

Later that evening while staring moonfully into one of the carpets I noticed an inscription. I had done as Basa had bid, and not only had I studied Khayyam's verses but I had begun translating them. I recited the verse aloud—

Iram indeed is gone with all its Rose,
And Jamshyd's Sev'n-ring'd Cup where no one knows.

At once the pattern in the first carpet began shimmering and oscillating. I gaped at this phenomenon, and to my bewilderment saw an image of Basa within the carpet's central design. I saw her, as if through a telescope, being guided by a young man, down the path of an ornate garden. I saw everything she had described to me—the whole story pictured within the patterns. First one carpet, then the next, would open its eye to reveal its visions. In the last carpet I witnessed the storm and its wrecking of the Dutch vessel. I watched myself bidding Basa farewell. Then the vision moved on to new territory, and I saw her leaving Suffolk and traveling to Sweden, where, after a protracted search, she cornered her nemesis in the grounds of a crumbling Malmo mansion. The images became shrouded in shadow and I could only just make out the long thin knife that Basa held by her side, as she silently stalked a hooded figure into the darkness of a rain-swept cedar grove.

For a while I stood in shock, then I returned to the first carpet and re-recited the verse that had triggered the story's beginning. The carpets remained motionless. I tried again and again. I lost my temper and cursed them, demanding that they show me more—I needed to see the outcome. But there was nothing more to see.

An overwhelming sense of loss assaulted me. I ran to the boathouse, I wanted to rig *Scandal*, and sail for Sweden. But I couldn't risk such a foolish act, so I returned to the house and the carpets.

For months, even though it was futile, I attempted to bring the carpets back to life. I was sure the key lay in the Khayyam translations, and I strove to uncover it. But in the end I gave up, for in truth, the verses always seemed as immutable as those blind eyes hanging from my walls.

The Moving Finger writes; and, having writ,
Moves on; nor all thy Piety nor Wit
Shall lure it back to cancel half a Line,
Nor all thy Tears wash out a Word of it.
         —Tamam Shud

It became clear to me that Fitzgerald's relationship with the carpets was traumatic; they inspired him, yet mocked his inability to break free from his ivory tower. He knew he had deserted his love, and had condemned himself to lifelong sadness—the comfortable familiarity of disappointment had been too tempting to turn his back on.

I am assured by my poetic advisers that the underlying fatalism of his Khayyam translations reflected Fitzgerald's outlook far more than it did the mysticism of the great Sufi poet and mathematician. (Personally I was fond of his verses—but then I am no judge.) Fitzgerald felt that his inability to understand the poems' subtleties had prevented him from finding the words to reopen the carpets' eyes.

Gazing again into the designs of the carpets, as they hung from the Museum's walls, he saw his missed opportunity. In failing to pursue Basa, he had failed himself. The soul that would have driven him had remained unheeded, and he had slipped into atrophy. In his final submission he acknowledged the faintness of his spirit, and resolved to stiffen his courage in one of the harsher Dystopias.

THE GAZIO ROOM

*T*he Gazio Room contains fifteen shrines and twenty-three boxes, conceived and constructed by Lizbeth Gazio, before and after her entry into Purgatory. Most of the shrines and boxes are made of wood, though the elements within them come from numerous sources. Broadly viewed I would describe them as icons, their cultural eclecticism embodying Gazio's affirmation that she was an inquisitive skeptic, as well as a travel addict.

Lizbeth had been a fidgety child, never still, always scratching at the walls and gazing longingly at the horizon. At nine, she began making endless lists of places, map coordinates, travel equipment, and invented timetables.

Born into a family of sixteen, suffocated by the poverty of her living conditions, and bursting with a need to explore, she ran away from home at the age of fourteen. She was skinny, precocious, had the knack of making friends easily, and found little difficulty in tracing her way around the countryside. Unfortunately (or fortunately) within a couple of years she blossomed into womanhood and her undisguisable good looks made her carefree existence progressively more precarious.

Shrines & Navigational Boxes

Irritated but unscathed, and determined to travel further afield, she was no longer willing to risk the road, and signed on as a maid on a passenger liner. The vessel was barely out of dock when the head steward set his sights on her, but before the self-styled Don Juan could exercise his seduction campaign, Lizbeth was swept away by the ship's captain, who courted and married her inside the week.

The captain loved cartography and was a collector of all manner of navigation matter. During their extensive journeying together, his enthusiasm for old maps and instruments filtered through to Lizbeth. When he died in a cargo accident on their tenth wedding anniversary, she was left as the keeper of his memory and his prodigious collection.

In the dozen or so years that followed, the winds took Gazio on a zig-zag course across the continents, drove her through three marriages and many love affairs. Despite a lack of material need, she found her liaisons providing her with a growing list of possessions, including figures of devotion from most of the major world faiths. These statues she kept safely, along with her other records of transit, instinctively knowing that one day she would find a use for them.

In her late thirties, Lizbeth's compulsion to travel was slowed by a broken pelvis, suffered in a fall from an elephant's howdah. Her minor internal injuries took a complicated turn for the

The Insight Box.

worse and any possibility that she might bear children was eradicated. During her convalescence she considered the implications of her barrenness, and decided to redirect her maternal instincts.

When her recovery was complete, Lizbeth moved to The Badlands, where she settled with an old lover, Mikael Swann. He was a philanthropist-carpenter and had just begun to build an orphanage. Lizbeth threw herself into Swann's project with all her customary enthusiasm and during the following few years learned the crafts of painting and carpentry. Together she and Swann created a children's home so spectacularly peculiar, it became known throughout the county as much for its appearance as its liberal kindnesses.

While helping to build the orphanage, she discovered, much to her surprise, that her journeyman's willingness to learn the techniques of construction had become a zeal for sculpture. Her drive to keep moving eased, and she was able to concentrate her energy into her new-found passion for boxes and shrines.

Content to be still (apart from the occasional walkabout), Lizbeth's preoccupation ran away with her, and when the orphanage staff settled in, she gave herself wholly over to her creations. Her travels had led her to believe in a spirituality devoid of boundaries. Her shrines, navigational boxes, and map cabinets enabled her to express her distinct sense of theological cross-pollination, as well as allowing her to make good use of her belongings.

Lizbeth Gazio described herself to me as an "unarriving traveler." She made fun of the ridiculousness of her innocent belief in good fortune, but never failed to acknowledge that her nomadic wanderings rewarded her in a way that no confirmed armchair traveler could ever imagine. (I could tell that her optimism and enthusiasm were completely genuine, and I must admit that irritated me; I was jealous of her and disliked myself for it.)

Although Lizbeth's compulsive moving habit had diminished, her memories remained intense. Her body may have grown tired, but her wanderlust merely reassigned itself to the metaphysics of art.

By the time she emerged from the Dreamwell, she had journeyed some way towards resolution. Her generosity and her warm nature showed a beguiling sense of trust. But the stumbling block she encountered proved to be her desire to move on from Purgatory—her rekindled eagerness to begin a new journey hindering her otherwise thorough self-assessment.

Once again she began building shrines and boxes. And by repeating the process she'd learned in the latter portion of her life, she was able to quell her impatience and calm her spirit. Lizbeth carefully examined the Utopian options, and in so doing gradually came to understand the enigmatic way in which her destination would select her, not she it.

The Elephant Box.

THIS PAGE: *Pandora's Travel Box. For Gazio, journeying meant an eruption of sensation. The Travel Box was to remind her to remain open-minded.*

FACING PAGE, LEFT: *Cosmologist's Box. Astrological belief has it that the greater (the macrocosm) is reflected in the lesser (the microcosm), hence Gazio's use of a star map and a magnifying glass.*

FACING PAGE, RIGHT: *Temptation Box. A half-naked, tattooed temptress swings high above a monk. The monk is futilely trying not to notice. Gazio believed that desire should lead to spiritual bliss, not keep one from it.*

*Gatehouse Shrine.
Gazio spent many
years in Indochina
and the Gatehouse
Shrine expressed her
affinity for the dancers
and spiritual crafts-
men of the region.*

*Black Angel Shrine.
This truly mongrel
work consists of a
Balinese collapsible
trumpet, a Chinese
angel made of iron,
carved wings from a
chair back, a New
Guinea squatting
stool, a Victorian
velvet curtain, and
a wooden machine
part from a North
American pulp mill.*

*Ganesha Shrine.
Even her near fatal
fall from the pachy-
derm's back couldn't
reduce Gazio's enthu-
siasm for building a
shrine honoring the
mischievous elephant
half-boy who cares for
the everyday needs of
ordinary people.*

*Penguin Lighthouse
Shrine. Lizbeth created
this tongue-in-cheek
phallus, to pay homage
to the lights of her life.
She preferred men with
a direct approach to
courtship, much like
the penguins who
express their desires by
placing carefully
selected stones in front
of desired mates.*

THE AMORFE ROOM

*T*here have been many fine works on entomology brought to Purgatory, but none better than Piatro Amorfe's drawings and photographs, depicting his unprecedented study of insect collaboration through the stages of amalgamation, biomechanic development, and industrial symbiotics.

This room contains both Amorfe's research drawings and the remains of his sadly eroded mountings.

Amorfe's influences were extreme—a father who built life-sized clockwork figures and a mother who dissected laboratory animals. It wasn't difficult for me to comprehend why young Piatro was drawn to the fusion of natural and engineering sciences in the form of entomechanics.

Amorfe grew up in particularly bewildering and unpleasant surroundings. His parents' love-hate relationship expressed itself in the form of violent physical argument and openly lustful reunion. Piatro's exposure to these oscillations left him highly confused. During the fights Amorfe would try to insert himself between the two grown-ups, hoping to stop them from killing one another. This desperate, appeasing tactic often led to Amorfe

Entomological Amalgams

incurring a second-hand beating of his own. When his parents were making up, and as he put it, "mauling each other disgustingly," he would try to disappear, but their tiny apartment left him nowhere to avoid the sights and sounds of their manic coupling.

Scarred by his experiences, his confidence took another slide during a short and disastrous liaison with an older cousin. Consequently Amorfe buried himself in his studies. Stripped of his defenses, he symbolically compensated by developing an intense interest in insect exoskeletal body armor. (On one occasion I encountered him, in an upper corridor of the Museum, with a large tortoise shell strapped to his back.)

Unfortunately his already fragile psyche could not cope with the demands he placed on himself, and the thousands of hours he spent holding his breath while he reconstructed and illustrated his imagined observations, finally unhinged him.

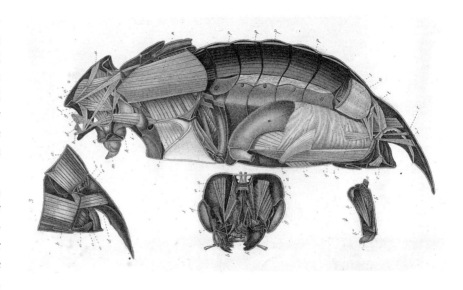

Armadillo beetle illustration.

As far as I can ascertain, the study of entomechanism and its metamorphoses was in fact Amorfe's own concept. He diligently observed, and meticulously recorded insect behavior for over thirty-five years, during which time he claimed he was constantly rebuffed and ignored by the scientific community. His counterparts concluded that his findings ran counter to all previous precepts.

According to Piatro Amorfe, the body of proof he'd gathered eventually became too monumental for his discoveries to be ignored. He said that, having established beyond question the borging capacity of certain insects, he was awarded the Nobel prize for entomology, and the following year was inducted into the entomological hall of fame.

Amorfe's insistences aside, there would seem to be a rather large discrepancy between our understanding of events, and his (the Museum, it should be pointed out, keeps extensive documentation on all of its visitors). He never was awarded the Nobel prize. In fact he never submitted his research to any of the formal scientific bodies, which is in many ways unfortunate because there are truths amongst his creations that might have enlightened a whole generation of insect behaviorists.

When I asked him about his treatment as a child, Amorfe repeatedly stated that, "Pain didn't matter, and that determination made him strong."

On another occasion I suggested that maybe his unconscious had pushed him to try to unify seemingly incompatible elements in his work. His response was aggressive: "As for the so-called unconscious, I have always considered *that* an invention of those wishing to be irresponsible!"

From the first, I had grave doubts about Amorfe's capacity to adjust to Purgatory. And when the subject of his bogus Nobel prize came up, I tried to suggest that it might be advisable if he took longer to reflect. But he became enraged, ranting that he didn't need to consider his life, it was an unmitigated success. He was a great man. He had work to do. He must get out of Purgatory immediately. He had to immerse himself in the insect world. He needed to know what it was like to spread his wings, grow antenna, twitch his proboscis.

Piatro Amorfe's capacity for self-delusion was an art in itself. Maybe I should have sanctioned a temporary restraint order (forced pacification by the administration of poppy juice), but it seemed pointless. Occasionally we get cases where imbalances are so profound that no amount of sedation will help. Then it becomes perspicacious to invoke "the direct transfer act," and place the being accordingly. In Amorfe's case, that meant the poignant choice of an Eden rebirth, in the guise of a Napoleon Dragonfly *(Anax Imperator).*

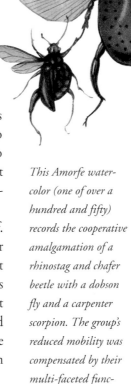

This Amorfe watercolor (one of over a hundred and fifty) records the cooperative amalgamation of a rhinostag and chafer beetle with a dobson fly and a carpenter scorpion. The group's reduced mobility was compensated by their multi-faceted functionalism.

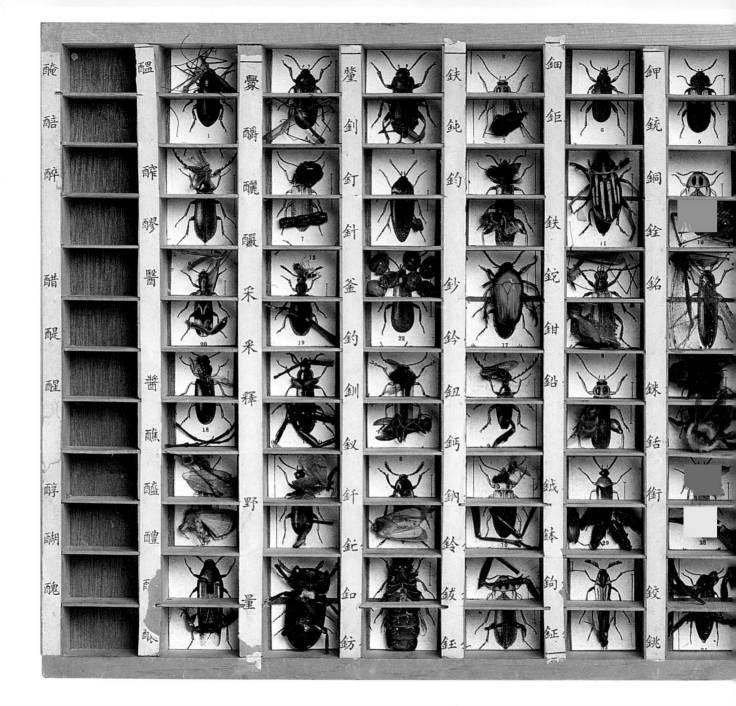

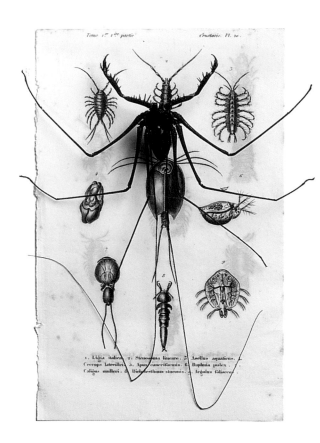

Amorfe took great pride in his photo-graphic studies of insects. This tailless scorpion has been carefully posed on top of one of Amorfe's simulated eighteenth-century engravings.

Amorfe kept his specimens and insect spare body parts in a cabinet built out of Chinese typesetting drawers. Each drawer was named after a well-known graveyard—this illustration depicts Highgate cemetery.

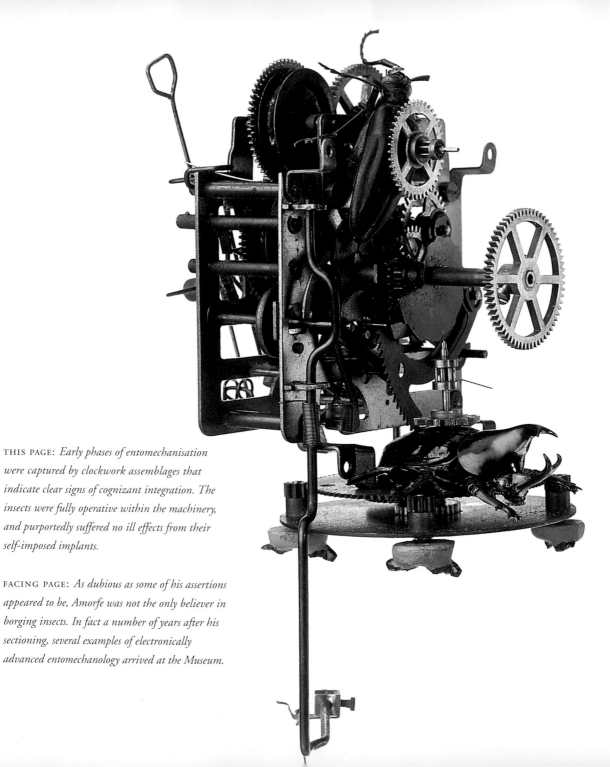

THIS PAGE: *Early phases of entomechanisation were captured by clockwork assemblages that indicate clear signs of cognizant integration. The insects were fully operative within the machinery, and purportedly suffered no ill effects from their self-imposed implants.*

FACING PAGE: *As dubious as some of his assertions appeared to be, Amorfe was not the only believer in borging insects. In fact a number of years after his sectioning, several examples of electronically advanced entomechanology arrived at the Museum.*

THE DELANCET ROOM

*T*he transportation of mail between the Utopian and Dystopian states, and the Standard Atlas Countries has always been somewhat convoluted. The Post Office at Purgatory plays no part in the sorting and distribution of this mail. However, as is the way with postal services, certain items become inadvertently displaced and as they cannot be returned or destroyed, they pass on to Purgatory by default, where they stay in long-term holding.

Delancet's exhibit focuses on the principal aspects of the postal system, and specifically the inbound correspondence describing the social and geographical climate within the Dystopian and Utopian communities.

When Eugene Delancet discovered that only one item from his mail collection had accompanied him after death he became distraught. Delancet simply found the thought of self-assessment too confusing, without his security blanket. His life-long study material was so necessary to his sense of continuity that he felt incapable of facing the problems before him.

To help reorient himself, I gave him permission to organize the Museum's collection of lost mail. This he did, taking the

Lost Post

The only surviving piece from Delancet's personal collection. *In January 1845, after complaints that paper stamps were easily torn and therefore inadmissible, the P.O. modified its strict ruling—permission was given for a pair of damaged stamps to be joined in a double bisect. But it soon became clear that cancels were being cut off and stamps re-used. Less than three months after the first edict, the Postmaster General rescinded the concession. In this rare Maltese cross example, a penny black and penny red have been combined.*

rag-bag of cards and letters, cataloguing and cross-referencing them, then creating the display that can be seen in the room that bears his name.

Delancet's parents were killed when he and his sister were in their early teens. The youths had always been close, but the reliance they were forced to invest in one another after their parents death lead inexorably to an intense and intimate relationship. (When Eugene came to this point in his narrative my curiosity became suddenly heightened. There seemed to me, a delicate sadness and excitement around the idea of consenting brother-sister sexuality.)

A tête-bêche pair of stamps issued by Inferno.

The wrench that Delancet experienced when he finally separated from his sister's company was profound. They attended universities on opposite sides of the country, writing to one another on a daily basis. He grew dependent on correspondence as a means of keeping at bay the depressions that threatened to engulf him. This reliance on the mail service gradually developed into an affinity with philatelic ephemera and led him to study and build a substantial collection of postal history.

Time and distance put an end to the siblings' physical relationship, but their link was such that they continued to correspond regularly for the rest of their lives. Brother and sister both married in mid-life, but neither revealed to their respective spouses the details of their adolescent years.

Having majored in criminal social history, Eugene was unable to gain employment within the education system and after a year of failed job applications, drifted into the business sector where he became an internal security analyst. At university he'd specialized in graphology and postal forgery. His employers paid him well for his services, and he was able to indulge in expanding his postal history collection still further. But with the passing of years he became progressively more uncomfortable living in the shadows of a clandestine corporate operation—he had spent too long keeping secrets and finally he quit his job. Wishing to remain within his realm of knowledge, he took his skills to The Letter Agency, and was rewarded

by being made the Assistant
Postminder General.

*Notice of increase
in railway tax
from Peridiqes in
Pandemonium.*

He and his sister had
in essence, been deserted
by their parents' demise.
Delancet's need for reassur-
ance was constant, and after
parting from his sibling,
he'd tried to create a chain
of letters, an umbilical cord
to his lost family. I could
tell that correspondence was
his lifeline, but could never
break the subconscious feeling that he had been cast adrift.

The peace Delancet found amongst the vaults of lost post
allowed him to see with perspective. In sorting through the mountain of paper, his panic calmed. He was able to acknowledge the
demands that loss and dependency had placed on both himself
and his sister, and that his subsequent addiction to secretiveness
was no more than a reflex action.

With those realizations Delancet was able to let go of his
incest guilt and feelings of desertion, accept the worth of his
hard work and diligence, and consider a replenishment program
in one of the pleasanter outer Utopian States.

BELOW: *Preprinted letter from Elderado [sic] to Novo Hamburgo, damaged by exposure to golddust.*

RIGHT: *Charity postcard from Styx River colonies, affixed with semi-postal sinking fund stamp.*

LEFT: *Shangri-la curled serpent overprint on Tibet stamp. Letter passed through Chinese postal check.*

BELOW: *Sealed photo-card sent to Luxor by Archelo Cavarn, showing Howard Carter on the steps of their dig in Falak al Aflak.*

ABOVE: *Card from Nirvana affixed with Nippon Official Mail (OM) tag.*

TOP LEFT: *Letter sent to Bethlehem in New Jerusalem, but addressed in error to Pennsylvania.*

TOP RIGHT: *Card from Terminus depicting Kaspare's defeat of the Schönberg dragon.*

BOTTOM: *Rocket Mail from Capolan, the vagabond Utopia, addressed to Atta Dijjo III, first Capalonian Secretary General of the U.N.*

```
                                   27.6.59

Re:Pocket Tour of Utopias
EDEN

With its copiously lush and verdant vegetation
Eden is truly a horticulturist's dream. Blessed
by an abundance of docile animals, including the
gentlest of lions and tigers, only the occasional
snake needs be watched out for.

    As for the Garden's food, you'll find it
delicious throughout. However you must remember
to steer clear of the black market fruit, it's
been known to have a powerful hallucinogenic
effect and the local constabulary have little
sympathy for those who become intoxicated. Believe
us when we say, this is not the kind of place you
want to get deported from.
PS. Don't forget, Eden is a clothes free zone,
so you'll have to be prepared to divest yourself
of your attire when passing through customs.
E.H.
```

ABOVE: *Lettergram
from a facile travel-
guide writer attempt-
ing to satirize
conditions in Eden.*

ABOVE AND RIGHT:
*Cover of a folded letter
from Satanic Mills
that contained an
underground newspa-
per clipping recording
a passage from Joseph
Swallow's revolution-
ary speech to the rebel
parliament, attacking
the conditions in the
State industrial quar-
ter. The KGC (King's
Government Censors)
confiscated the letter
and held it until the
hundred year ruling
had elapsed.*

SWALLOW'S NOBLE DECLARATION

Within the heart of our beloved Albion lies a separate and isolate country, a dark and terrible land beyond sunlight's penetration. Forever shrouded in a putrid fog, its gargantuan soot-saturated factories dwarf into irrelevance all human life. For those poor drones unlucky enough to have been cast into the mills there is no hope of reprieve. It is their lot to die young, a miserable and painful death, only to be reborn again within their childrens' bodies, where they will grow merely to continue the merciless cycle of drudgery.

    Can it be that we will continue to turn our backs on the plight of these pitiful peoples, or will we rise up and say, "The fate of our brothers and sisters today, may yet be our fate tomorrow. Enough is enough. Let us tear asunder the odious walls and liberate those within." +

BELOW: *Exposition card celebrating the reopening of Avalon's Gate. Posted Roma Centro, Heaven.*

ABOVE: *Registered letter from Samuel Braithweight to his granddaughter Josephine, containing a picture and belated confirmation of safe arrival in Fiddler's Green. Sent to Karaaikudi, returned to Fiddler's Green, patched on, undelivered and finally consigned to the post office at Purgatory. Included in the letter is the following informative account of Braithweight's first moments in the Sailor's Utopia—*

". . . it were round noontime when I come upon the village, serene it were and dappled in sunlight. So I stopped, and rested myself on the bench outside the Pig and Whistle. I lit my pipe and greeted the passersby and they in turn greeted me with friendly smiles.

I were preparin' to move on when a young maid dressed all in white walked up to me and said, 'Please sir, tell me what be you carryin' 'cross your shoulder?'

With tears in my eyes I replied the traditional reply, 'Why my dear, that is an oar.' And, as I uttered those words, I watched the inn door slowly swing open, revealing my old shipmates who toasted my health and welcomed me to Fiddler's Green."

TOP LEFT: *Letter to the Museum Curator, posted locally in Purgatory.*

TOP RIGHT: *Invoice sent from an Austrian brewer to the quartermaster at Valhalla requesting payment for a shipment of twenty flagons of Gösser ale.*

CENTER: *Misdirected cyphergram from Olympus.*

BOTTOM: *Small envelope posted in Hades, sent to Marseilles, in Avalon, retrieved damaged from hot-air balloon crash.*

THE NATHIUS ROOM

Visitors to Purgatory have spawned many inventive activities to occupy themselves while their transfers remained pending, and at the Museum we have a full collection of these entertainments on display. The Nathius room contains the works of the most prolific inventor of unconventional games—Garrik Nathius.

The board and card games that Nathius contrived varied enormously, from the natural simplicity of *Pangur Ban* to the highly complex *Termini,* from the frantic gambling game *On the Nail* to the esoteric *Aurio Sectio.*

Throughout his early boyhood Garrik Nathius seemed lethargic and of an unexcitable countenance. His only real interest was dominoes, a game taught to him (as soon as his hands were large enough to grip the pieces) by his seafaring uncle. His parents put Garrik's apparent tardiness down to a lack of friends or siblings, but unbeknownst to them his problem, and solution, lay within his body.

Garrik contracted glandular fever at the age of eleven, the same year that the local school burned down. Without companions

Games

and forced into house quarantine, he began playing a domino marathon against a non-existent foe. Four days into the game, the results of Garrik's chest X-ray (undergone to establish the cause of his lingering malaise) came back from the laboratories. And something remarkable was revealed in Nathius' torso. Inside his right lung the doctors discovered Garrik's twin brother—a tiny, perfectly preserved, lifeless fetus. Garrik became upset when told of the discovery, believing that his new brother would be taken from him. But, as the three-inch-long twin offered no threat to Garrik's well being, the physicians decided against an operation, and the brothers were left intact.

The knowledge that he had an internal twin had a strangely galvanizing effect on Garrik; he perceived his brother to be a rival. He named him Kirch, and set about devising ways to compete with his ever-present companion. (Unlike Delancet's feelings towards his sister, I sensed Nathius had little sentiment for his brother. His only desire was to outsmart him.)

Seeing Garrik return to his domino marathon worried his mollycoddling mother. She fretted that his recovery might be retarded by boredom and suggested that he try inventing new games of his own, rather than playing the same one repeatedly. Little could she have known that Garrik would never again be bored—he had already found a lifelong companion and opponent.

Translucent onyx dice used in the Fenian storytelling game Tinker's Cuss.

Fighting Samourai Tops, *a Nathius game designed under commission by Matrice Levant.*

Her intervention sowed a unexpectedly fertile seed. Nathius switched from playing to making, and driven by an energy previously untapped he and Kirch constructed numerous intricate games. Many of his creations were manufactured and sold before he was out of his teens, and he was running a large and highly profitable game company by the age of twenty-five.

His ongoing brotherly battlings drew Garrik deep into this world of play, where he found a lucrative career and a means of self-expression. But his need to outwit his twin could not be satiated, and he continually required new fields of competition, new opportunities for winning. He even structured his company as a partnership, allotting half his invented games to Kirch, in the hope that his own projects might accrue more revenue than his brother's.

Garrik's ultimate pursuit was the perfect game. In his senior years, with the company in the hands of his children, he turned his attention to higher thoughts, and spent his days trying to refine his metaphysical game *Commedia dell' Alchemic.* Even after his passing, he continued to invent and devise playful distractions like *Descent from Purgatory* and *Tantra.*

To their grave, Garrik and Kirch remained permanently locked in inseparable combat.

While competitiveness in itself is not stultifying, the degree to which Garrik pursued his quest clearly inhibited his potential to relate meaningfully to anyone or anything outside the reflection he held within. He was too cunning for his own good. On some level he understood that his compulsion to continually beat Kirch was a futile nonsense, but he cultivated his obsessive behavior to push himself though life.

(Neutrality aside, Nathius got on my nerves. I liked his games, but as a person I experienced him as humorless and evasive. I had to work extremely hard to get him to separate into singularity, and even after he'd acknowledged his preoccupation he found it difficult not to measure himself against his brother's imagined prowess.)

When Garrick finally stood back from Kirch, the magnitude of his self-preoccupied blinkardness seemed staggering and it became plain to him that in his next placement he would have to deal with his self-assertion externally. Preferably in a game-free Dystopian State.

Early Sasak, *dual-purpose calendar and horse racing game.*

Tantra

When Nathius first created Tantra *(originally called "Carnal Knowledge") it was a game of sexual titillation that reflected the recreational attitude towards sex that was in vogue at the time. After his death, he redesigned the game's rules to bring them into line with his new surroundings. Sex in Purgatory is a matter of passionate meditation, not lust, which for Nathius proved to be somewhat of a revelation.*

Wishing to redress the crudeness of his past attitudes, and to honor a Tantric perception of sensuality, he renamed his old game. In Tantra *the board functions as a mandala, and the track records the initiates' progress as they travel in opposite directions around the perimeter (passing twice on each cycle). Only when the couple land on the same square does congress take place—thus allowing chance rather than desire to decide the moment of union.*

Commedia dell' Alchemic

Nathius had a fondness for wordplay and music, and in the Commedia, *a board game of pantomime and ritual chemistry, he indulged both.*

The illustration shows the top left sixteenth of the gameboard. All the familiar figures of the pantomime, including Pierrot, the Doctor and the other Zanies, are seen cavorting around the board's perimeter, along with the more enigmatic elements of the alchemical universe. Glass files of colored bronze function as markers. Players' moves are determined by adding the individual didgets of randomly selected prime numbers. The inner section of the board represents the cosmos. Note the holy cows strolling amongst the heavenly pillars.

The game plays on the word "base." From base metal comes the search for purification. From base behavior comes the filter of experience. Nathius reminds himself and his fellow Purgatorians that their crude selves must be accepted along with their desire for higher values. Even the prerequisite musical accompaniment is carefully linked by wordplay. The two instruments required being the lute (money) and the flute (a lute, fronted by a bass [base] clef).

Pangur Ban

Pangur Ban *was based on a tiger-stalking game invented in India by a company of Welsh dragons. The name "Pangur Ban" comes, not from the Indian sub-continent, but from an eighth-century cat poem found in a Carinthian monastery. Early boards and pieces, like the one shown here, were native carved. Later, as the game became popular throughout Europe, it passed through numerous stylistic and rule changes.*

On The Nail

On The Nail *is an addictive gambling game favored by those Purgatorians whose lifestyle suggested that their final Dystopian destination would almost inevitably be a Styx paddle steamer. The rules require players to compete to avoid the inevitability of diminishing resources. The original game takes its name from the nail-shaped bollard on the Bristol dockyards that was used as a bargaining table for much of Europe's slave trading.*

RIGHT, TOP TO BOTTOM: *Scoreboard configurator, Germanic deco; marker pegs; eighteenth-century deal block (the design of the nail or frogge in the center of the block was later appropriated for the less frenetic purposes of stabilizing flower arrangements).*

FAR RIGHT: *Half-sized gambling bank notes.*

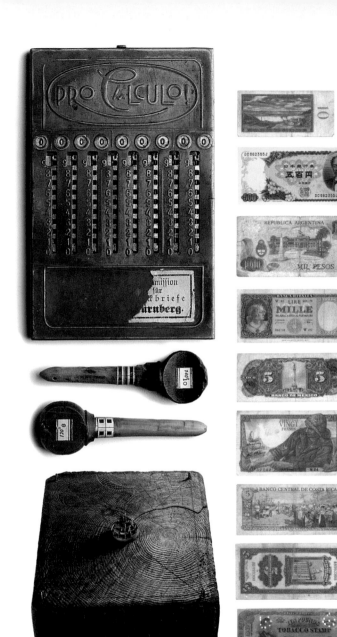

Aurio Sectio

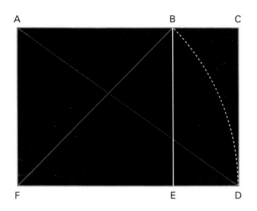

Aurio Sectio is *a Game of Balance. There is a place on any line where the ratio of the smaller part to the larger is the same as the larger part to the whole. The ancients called this place of division* aurio sectio. Aurio sectio *sits at the core of our perception of aesthetic beauty and innately governs the composition of most art and architecture. As a mathematical formula it can be used to describe both sea shells and spiral galaxies, yet it needs no calculation to define its placement. Within each of us lies the ability to locate its position precisely.*

Starting from separate posts (AD), *two blindfolded players set out to find the perfect spot between their respective home bases. Players are obliged to come to a standstill as close to the* aurio sectio *as they can. They may do this in isolation or by cooperation.*

Although Nathius described it as a game of pure intuition, he felt obliged to define the sequential construction of the playing field—ABFE: *the square;* FB: *the diagonal;* BD: *the arc;* ACDF: *the court;* AD: *the playing line.*

Descent from Purgatory

In this humorous card game for children, players are required to complete a row of lost souls who follow one another for a reason unknown. The game has an alphabetically alliterated rhythm meant to exploit a wide spectrum of tongue gymnastics. It is also a lesson in self-determination in which twenty-six creatures follow the lead soul who has no idea where it's going.

Nathius conceived the game after a discussion with Peter Bruegel—painter of "The Blind Leading the Blind."

Illred the Illbred — followed. . .

Jarub El Jud — followed. . .

Zeberdy Zeestaker — who is totally lost.

Quatro

Quatro *was Nathius' first success. Later he reflected that its popularity lay in cause and counter effect, players having to deal with the problems created by advancing an opponent's standing each time they improved their own.*

THE RULES: *Two players red and green, each gets 12 identical pieces—5 quatros, 5 duos, and 2 monos. The players take alternate turns placing their pieces on the board: the quatros, the duos, and finally the monos.*

The purpose of the game is to make paths and enclosures. A path is formed when a player completes a row of 3 or 4 spots or stripes, or a diagonal line of 4 or more of their own color. An enclosure is formed when a color is surrounded on all four sides by the opponent's color. When the board is filled the winner is the player that has the most points.

SCORING: *A horizontal or vertical path of 3 gets 6 points, a path of 4 gets 10 points. A diagonal path of 4 gets 4 points, a diagonal path of 5 gets 5 points and a diagonal path of 6 wins the game outright. Each enclosure entitles the player to deduct 1 point from their opponent's score.*

Partially completed
Quatro *game.*

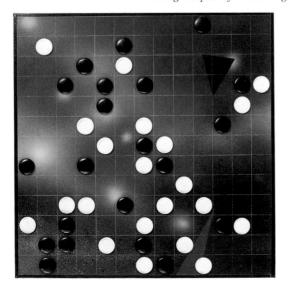

Termini

Similar in format to Go, black-and-white stones try to surround one another. However, in Termini the odds are stacked and white can never win. The game simply requires white to hold out against the dark tide as long as it can. Although the names of the Dystopian States would have been unknown to Nathius during his life, the game bears a striking similarity to the degenerated conditions in Termini itself.

THE LEVANT ROOM

Matrice Levant was a Renaissance throwback, a craftsman-artist with an unbridled curiosity for the physical sciences. He was fascinated by gravity, and while studying gyroscopics became interested in spinning tops, creating designs for a variety of centrifugal rotators of an elaborate nature. The pure artistic potential of spinning tops captured him, and before long he found himself on a trail that would inadvertently set in motion an anarchic hoax of bizarre proportion.

As Levant's preoccupation with spinning tops grew he started to consider their unfulfilled historical potential—he mused on the idea that our ancestors had failed to take the opportunity of raising the rotator to a place of social significance. Unable to leave well alone, Levant's mischievous temperament demanded that he correct the past, so he set out to manufacture a selection of tops that might have existed, but didn't.

Once his satisfyingly complex lineage had been constructed, he wrote an imagined account on the subject, and idly sent his *Short History of Spinning Tops* to an eminent publisher. A few weeks later, he was surprised to be offered a contract. But that

Spinning Tops

was nothing compared to his astonishment when he realized the publisher perceived his indulgence to be a work of non-fiction. He wondered how long it would take for the masque to be exposed. But it never was. The book was a success, running to a second and third printing, and soon artifact collectors from around the world were searching for examples of ancient and classic spinning tops.

Levant admitted to me that he'd considered the possibility of owning up to the deception, but as he hadn't initially intended to obscure the truth—and, for that matter, had found the whole thing thoroughly amusing—he'd decided to let the farce run its course.

After he'd created a surge of intense interest in a figment of his imagination, he couldn't resist the idea of supplying the market demand with his own tops. He didn't search out buyers, but when people pursued him and insisted he part with one of his brood, he simply acquiesced. When enough serious collectors and art galleries had purchased his tops the cozenage was sealed, and any notion that the tops might be revealed as modern fabrications became out of the question. Soon, museums from all nations were touting not only Levant's suitably aged creations, but any manner of dubious objects resurrected from their storerooms that could be cited as examples of early tops.

The hoaxer looked on in ever increasing wonder, as his version of history started to merge seamlessly with the past, until

Figure 1

Figure 2

eventually it became an integral part of the anthropological establishment. (Levant's hoodwinking of authority pleased me enormously. I couldn't of course show this, but internally I applauded every act of his deception.)

Unlike Piatro Amorfe, Levant's childhood wasn't unpleasant, it simply lacked the basic constituent of parental affirmation. His mother and father were, to all intent and purpose, strangers—a diplomat and his wife, who, when in the same time zone, would pat the young Matrice on the head and kiss him a hasty goodnight. Levant was brought up by a string of colorless governesses whose combined intelligences failed to add up to that of the boy's. He learned there were advantages to keeping up his guard and showing little emotion. He feigned laziness, and appeared indifferent, yet when alone, his world was alive with all manner of wild experiments, construction, art books, and painting materials.

Levant never withdrew completely, nor did he sour; he remained self-contained and ready to open up when the time was ripe. Coming of age freed him from his family constrictions, and he entered into society with enthusiasm, bringing with him a well-developed sense of irony.

After the furor of the spinning top extravaganza Levant attempted to stay out of the limelight, but he had established himself in a way that was difficult to avoid. The celebrity he engendered combined with his good breeding, guaranteed him a high profile. Eventually he became a consultant for the great museums, a role he accepted predominantly to allow himself to instigate further occasional acts of rebellious deception.

Levant married at thirty, fathered five children who he lavished with much attention, and spent his free time patenting and exhibiting sublimely noncognitive inventions such as *the protracted suction wheel* and *the combine matrix detacher*.

I tend to concur with Levant's view—history is a matter of interpretation, and although he stretched that premise to its full, his contrived chronology of spinning tops can hardly be said to have done harm.

When I asked about forgery, he responded, "I didn't forge, I copied no one. I faked the past, tweaking and distorting what was already there. I knew what I was doing, I knew the chaos I was creating and I was quietly delighted by it. I admit, the enjoyment I gleaned from the whole enterprise troubled me somewhat. When it came to self-adjudication I needed to decide whether I had taken pleasure at the expense of others, or had I simply exposed vanity and pomposity? In the end I concluded that it was an ethical question beyond my realm. My soul was my guide. It led me, and I followed—I trusted its instinct then, and I trust it still."

Not wishing to hurry his departure to his next life, Matrice Levant subsequently applied to and joined Purgatory's Security Agency, where his skills were put to use in the Serious Forgeries Division.

Figure 3

Figure 4

(Figures 1 to 4: Designs attributed to Levant's pseudonyms.)

Levant's History of Spinning Tops

Shortly after discovering the Carmagh Spinning Stones, Thomas Westgatner, the eminent archaeologist, made the bold, and possibly reckless, statement that he had discovered the world's first toys.

Whether he was correct in his conclusions is a matter of conjecture. Certainly the diversity of topographies where spinning tops have been unearthed (from Aztec temples to Roman baths) suggests very early origins. Yet there really is no proof that these tops belonged to children. It is impossible to know for certain if the Carmagh tops were actually toys; they could equally have been gaming devices, methods of divination, or tools of ceremony.

The exhibit begins with the famous Sicmon Island Ceremonial Spinning Wheels. Like the Carmagh Stones, their beginnings may be misty, but their purpose and recent lineage are well documented.

Even better recorded are the *modern* spinning tops, which may be separated into two (sometimes overlapping) genres: the plaything and the art object.

In 1850 there began a trend, pioneered by Bartholomew Wiltshire, of factory-fashioned spinning tops. However, as with so many innovations it was not Wiltshire who benefited from the ensuing craze, but the entrepreneurs who followed him.

By 1900 the spinning top as a toy had lost its pull over the junior public imagination, yet the spinning top's extinction was saved through a new generation of designers and craftspeople who took the form as a means of self expression. These artisans brought with them a fresh spirit of enthusiasm, as well as an array of previously unexplored techniques and materials. Thus was born "the golden age of tops," a period that is well represented throughout this exhibit.

Musak Whipping Top, wood and clay.

Sicmon Spirit Wheel 1. Dried fungus, gourd, hob-stick and feathers.

The Sicmon Islands
early 19th century

The Sicmon ceremonial spinning tops were first recorded by Charles Darwin in his *Beagle Diaries.*

According to the islands' inhabitants, elders have always made spirit wheels; they are an integral part of a Sicmon Islander's coming of age ceremony. Forty-nine tops, one for each year of the initiate's age, are simultaneously danced off a tiny pier-like structure into the ocean.

Sicmon Spirit Wheel 2. *Sand-dollar, hob-stick, brass (flotsam) and Boni feathers.*

Bartholomew Wiltshire
1828–1887

Born in Bradford, Bartholomew Wiltshire made his living as an engineer. He was the first to manufacture spinning tops for the mass market. However, his tops, which were cast iron, never found popular favor as they were overly heavy and tended to gouge grooves in the polished table surfaces they were spun on.

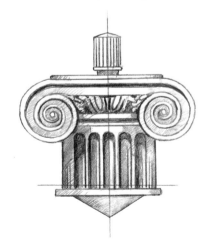

The Ionic Anvil. *Cast iron.*

Anna De Forte
1895–1942

Unquestionably the best of the Art Deco spinning top designers, Anna De Forte created tops laden with an inimitable sophistication. De Forte inherited her family fortune when only sixteen, and used her privilege to expand her artistic talents. She was coached by the best crafts-men in her native land and, by her mid-twenties, totally overshadowed her peers.

Firefly. *Hollowed silver weighted with lead.*

Jessica St. Paul
1887–1953

Of both Gaelic and native Indian ancestry, St. Paul grew up disliking and mistrusting humans. By nineteen she was a hermit, living in the forests of western Vancouver Island. While clearing her cabin, after her death in 1953, officials came upon a large pine chest containing hundreds of care-fully crafted ceremonial tops. What induced her to make them is unknown.

Foxwood Totem. *Shell, foxwood and hemp.*

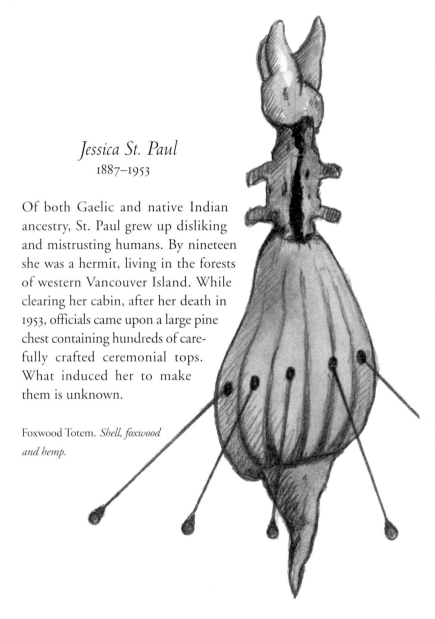

Gunter Mark
1901–1945

Mark was an idealist and his tops were rarely spinnable. They looked reasonable enough but his appalling sense of balance led him to consistently produce objects that would keel over within seconds. For years, he doggedly flogged at his chosen art but eventually his litany of failures began to topple his mind. He died in a drunken stupor, in spring 1945, while trying to descend a spiral staircase.

Caxon's Screw. *Brass.*

Thomas Ellis
1903–1929

Although under age, Ellis flew as a fighter pilot during the last two years of the Globe Wars. In the spring of 1919, he suffered a near-fatal crash and lost both his legs. Having been given only a short time to live, he was sent back to Old Hampshire to die quietly. But he clung to life for a further ten years, spending his time constructing his trademark "aviation spinners."

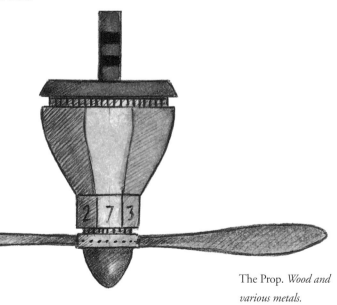

The Prop. *Wood and various metals.*

William Tosh
1916–1972

Grandson of the renowned Charles Rennie Tosh, William was an accomplished artist and designer in his own right. His interest in tops was short-lived, but in a five-year period between 1949 and 1954 he made over fifty beautiful and unique spinners.

The Fife Flyer. *Steel and etched ivory.*

Martin Porcubus
1928–

Porcubus was a student of William Tosh and his designs echo his master's style. Indeed, he still gives his tops the names of steam engines, as a mark of respect. In recent years he's begun to experiment with modern materials such as fiberglass, but by his own confession he is a traditionalist. He continues to build tops from his attic studio in Lisbon.

The Raith Whistle. *Teak, copper, china, bone, and polished coal.*

THE SENGLER ROOM

O tto Sengler's collection of calligraphic, petroglyphic, and hieroglyphic markings on stone, wood, paper, and animal skin were gathered specifically to support his views on the evolution of writing and its relationship to dream images.

Living on the Magya Steppes until he was fifteen, Sengler's formal education was virtually non-existent. Shortly after his family moved to the capital he determined to cultivate his mind and camped in the city library. When he reemerged three years later, he was brim-full with an eccentric mixture of fact and functionalism.

Of the vast quantity of books he devoured during his library siege, one in particular stood out—a short text on dream analysis. It contained a quote that stayed with him all his life: "We do not have dreams; dreams have us. Being illogical, they promote the sense in nonsense, and the straight-faced humor that that evokes. Our health relies on the playful way that dreams reflect back the edges of our egos, bolstering our sagging self-confidence when the all-too-serious universe suggests that we among all mortals are at fault."

Sfumatoglyphics

Each time he read the passage he became more interested in the fundamental discrepancy between the text he was reading and the subject matter's visual origins. He set out to try to develop an understanding of the tantalizingly elusive links between words and images.

For many years Sengler studied picturegrams and the birth of text, trying to equate the connections between these two tools of comprehension. He became unofficially involved in the research program that was conducting experiments into dream-language, at Standow University, and it was there that he began formulating the theoretical overview he later called Sfumatoglyphics.

Sengler's various treatises on Sfumatoglyphics (literally translated the word means smoky word pictures) were thoroughly researched and took a quarter of a century to bring together, but his lack of qualifications meant that his conclusions would receive little consideration from academic circles. So he took the only course open to him and set himself the target of writing about his subject in a populist form. Even that approach would have probably failed had he not struck on the idea of superimposing the text of his book over a series of running dreamscape images, thus bringing

Masonic petroglyph representing the power to float. The painted figures are identified with liberation from earthly restriction.

together message and symbol in a form not dissimilar to the way in which the brain deals with the simultaneous reception of a film's sounds and images.

During one of our conferences Sengler explained that for decades he worked himself mercilessly (only once did he break off, and that was in order to marry his doting, longtime assistant), trying to consolidate his theories and eager to show that a person cannot fully understand his own presence, unless he unites his two major means of visual perception.

The release of his theories in *The Sfumatoglyphic* brought popular acclaim, and later a begrudging recognition from The Academy. Yet for all the credit Sengler received, his origins made it difficult for him to accept the validity of his convictions. He criticized his own thoughts and ideas, saying they weren't backed by sound methodology, maintaining that his intuitive conclusions were convincing only because of the desperately distraught state of our society. (I pointed out that he'd revealed many truths and that he could hardly be blamed for being unaware of the Dreamwell and its influences. However, if he still wished to berate himself, that was his choice.)

Sengler was insecure, yet he'd managed to channel his fears towards a search for knowledge (unlike my insecurity which had culminated in the mistreatment of Marie Louise Gornier). Everything he espoused, supported the notion that understanding does not begin in formal learning. Even so, he was unable to

shake a deep rooted anxiety that his lack of formal education would be exposed and all of his subsequent work rendered irrelevant.

In Purgatory qualifications mean nothing. Nor is the city fooled by overblown humility born out of self-pity.

Finally, after much flagellation, Otto Sengler came to experience himself without pretensions, and to forgive the ignorance that was not individual but universal.

When his fear of failure lifted, he was able to consider his years of hard work favorably and thus permit himself to examine the pleasant possibilities of a Utopian sabbatical.

*C*onsider the following example of arbitrary language formation, and the confusion rendered by the perversity of words—

While wandering down a narrow alley beside the steep walls of one of the great Paris churches, James Boswell heard a blood-curdling noise coming from on high. Instinctively he looked up and saw a vile open-mouthed gargoyle, jutting from the church's gutter. He stood stock still, watching and listening to what appeared to be a stone beast's foul invective. Eventually his line of vision became interrupted by a more earthly face. A priest who had been swilling his throat with a garlic septic, stuck his head and torso out of a middle story window and discarded his mouthwash on the unnoticed traveler below.

Upset as Boswell was at receiving an unasked for bath, he took out his notebook and recorded the incident. Unfortunately the paper had also been splattered and his damp writing became blotchy. When he returned to England he did as he always did and passed his travel notes over to his good friend Dr. Johnson, who was in the habit of scouring any text to find material for his forthcoming dictionary.

A few days later while perusing Boswell's scribblings, Johnson came to the page containing the note about the priest and the gargoyle. Johnson was quite unaware that splatters from a human water spout had erased the letters *oy* from garg*oy*le and thinking he had come upon further depths of Boswell's vocabulary, added the word gargle to his list of dictionary inclusions. So the verb to gargoyle, which did not exist, was inadvertently changed to gargle. Thus becoming, probably, the only word in the English language to become corrupted at the moment of its birth.

FROM *Sfumatoglyphics* BY OTTO SENGLER

Before text, our ancestors existed in a realm of pictures, mental and physical. Their dream life and waking life were essentially made of the same components.

Writing's infancy came in the form of pictures. Later those images became simplified into picturegrams, which in turn became further stylized into symbols, and finally emerged as abstract text formations. These written abstractions are certainly adaptable, they allow us to express many complex notions, however they have isolated us from our picture-mind. Images are more allusive and elusive than text, and so they have gradually became a secondary means of communication. (There are many elements bolstering this transition, including the social-political control needed by paternalistic religions to supplement the polaristic views of right and wrong.)

This view of a dislocated psyche brings into question the degree to which our needs can be represented by the written word. Are our souls stranded, unable to express themselves in a suitable language? We don't dream in words, our imaginations are picture based. Images are multi-faceted and when combined with other of their like, offer multiple possibilities that become so dense they are only negotiable by means of intuition. They are non-quantifiable, therefore they appear to be unreliable. That's why our overt commitment to linear logic moves us away from an understanding of images.

We live by the word, which we can define and contain. But we are not content, we are unsettled. As adults we never feel properly heard and seen. This is hardly surprising, because we have become separated from the pictures that are the wellsprings of our being.

It would seem that few people today feel truly comfortable with images—our dream lives have become, at worst disowned, and at best clinically observed phenomena.

When word and picture marry, left and right brain operate simultaneously and a means of expression is available that offers far more than the limited view of existence we have become used to. The union provides a meeting ground where our two primary methods of observing reality can coexist.

—Excerpt from the opening of Otto Sengler's *The Closed Door.*

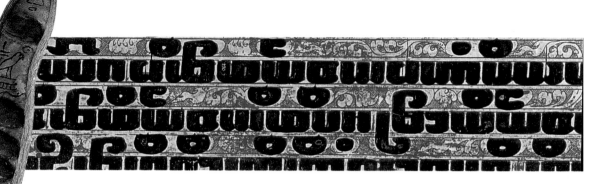

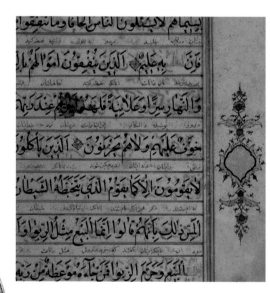

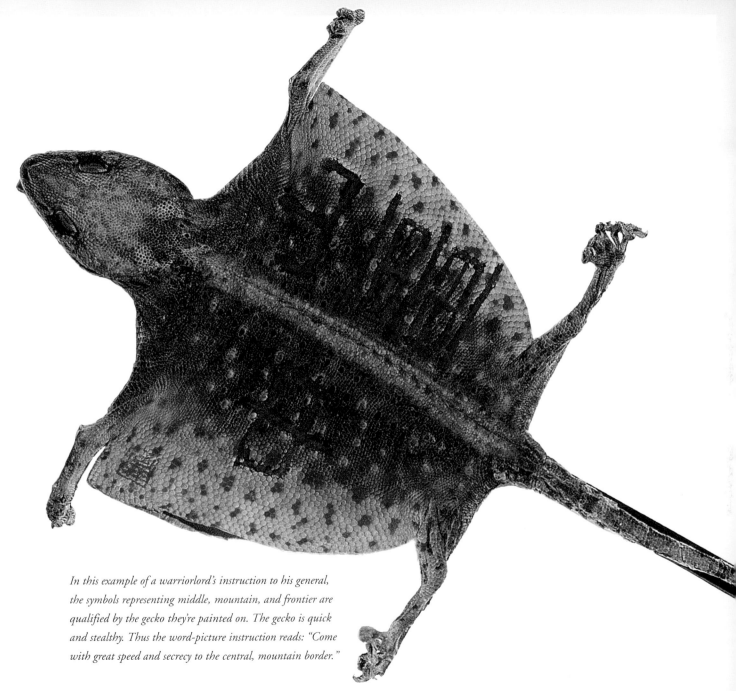

In this example of a warriorlord's instruction to his general, the symbols representing middle, mountain, and frontier are qualified by the gecko they're painted on. The gecko is quick and stealthy. Thus the word-picture instruction reads: "Come with great speed and secrecy to the central, mountain border."

SENGLER   77

THE CAVARN ROOM

Professor Archelo Bora Cavarn, the renowned archeologist, had the somewhat disturbing habit of walking around her university campus backwards—a peculiarity developed not to gain a reputation of eccentricity but to remind her students that the past should always be observed.

Cavarn's archeological exploits first came to notice some fifty years earlier, when she discovered the diminutive sarcophagi of Saratoa. Later, after the Amrah tomb was unearthed at Belshatha, and her theories on miniaturized mummies were proven correct, she found herself at the center of an international spotlight. Cavarn had headed the Belshatha dig herself, and the subsequent magnificence of the tomb's contents only added to the kudos her name had previously attracted.

Along with many perfect examples of shrunken mummies, the Belshatha find contained hieroglyphic proof that mummification of shrunken figures had been outlawed by the high priests of the Old Kingdom. The tomb's murals graphically showed that those heretics found infringing the deities' rights had been dealt with mercilessly. Yet, even the King's right hand

Miniature Mummies

could not stop the covert acts of reduction and embalment that one sect believed paved a way for slaves and animals to enter into the afterlife.

This particular sect was convinced that the miniature figures would find transportation into the afterworld more easily. The effectiveness of the practice seems proven by the quantity of these miniatures that I've noticed seeping into Purgatory. In fact, when Cavarn arrived in the city she was able to gather together many of the tiny mummies she'd once studied in Belshatha.

Cavarn's passion for archeology developed early, fixing her future occupation and her destiny. On leaving school she rejected the notion of college, preferring instead to learn her profession in the field. Working under some of the best archeologists of the day, she developed both practical knowledge and a selection of radical notions. One of these ideas, developed by linking a series of seemingly unrelated tomb inscriptions in the Souli desert, led her to the conviction that an excavation in Belshatha would provide the finds she was looking for.

With the financial help of her husband Jean de Teligon, Cavarn began the search that would take five

Oval haloskin from the lion statue surmounting the central dais of Amrah.

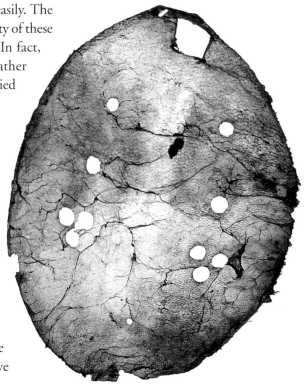

hard years and finally end in triumph. The discovery in Belshatha gave her a place in the archeological history books, but it brought with it many distractions. It seemed to Archelo that everyone, from the omnipresent press to the curious socialites who were arriving at the site in droves, wished to discuss the tomb and its contents. Just dealing with the questions ate up far more of her time than she could possibly afford to give.

The study and disassembling of the tomb absorbed Cavarn for the next ten years, though the constant bickering with the local authorities over exhibiting rights, slowed the process woefully. Cavarn was a stickler for detail, and would release nothing until it had been thoroughly examined and documented. Eventually this intractability, which had won her numerous minor battles, cost her the war and she was expelled from the country. Fortunately for Cavarn, de Teligon's old friend Victor Sorenson came to the rescue by making a second discovery of miniatures in Northern Rhodestaan. Cavarn headed straight there, and in the subsequent months was able to confirm a great deal that had until that point been only partially substantiated.

Cavarn spent a further forty years in various isolated locations before returning to her homeland, where she was heralded as the world's leading expert on mummification. She died and was embalmed a few days after her one hundred and second birthday.

Close observation of a passion often reveals the panic that feeds it. Archelo Cavarn's fondness for the past came directly from a fear of what was to come—a fear born out of a forgotten childhood misunderstanding. One day, overhearing her mother in the conservatory, tearfully lamenting the death of the fuchsia, Archelo thought she understood her parent to be saying, "The future is dead." And from this casual confusion she concluded that she had better stick to the past which was, no doubt, still alive. Strangely this error caused her no serious debilitation, although it did throw her equilibrium marginally out of kilter.

Cavarn's stippled ink and wash study of the Belshatha Bast.

By spending time in the Museum, Cavarn was able to see change in a different light. I encouraged her to watch the city and the souls within pass through their turns and transformations, thus she was able to rid herself of her preoccupation with holding back time. Even her precious talismen, the shrunken mummies, lost their hold over her, and she was able to travel on from Purgatory to the State of Falak al Aflak, where excavations into the future were already underway.

PREVIOUS PAGE:
Diminutive triple sarcophagi found in Saratoa. Figures from left to right: Mana Ra, Pfatii, and Buul. Side view of Buul.

RIGHT: *Type four chrysalis mummy with beeswax coating. The cartouche indicated a female human, but x-rays revealed a monkey.*

BELOW: *Gold breastplated Tuhmaren dog figure discovered in the Amrah tomb's inner chamber. The Dogman was supposedly a loyal and ferocious guard who would bite off the extremities of any thieves attempting to plunder the tomb.*

RIGHT: *Mummified, shrunken, and gilded Roc egg (height 10.5 cm). One of three found in North Rhodestaan by Victor Sorenson. In their original state, Roc eggs stand between 60 and 100 cm high.*

THE DANIEL ROOM

I submit that while no family can be wholly free from strife, there are some who maintain an even, unthreatening unity that allows its young to grow without the disruptions of shock. Renee Daniel came from such a family, and her daily routines reflected the orderly functionings of her unhindered mind and waifish body. Thus she was totally unprepared for the changes that swept through her with the onset of puberty.

The first visions came to her as slight, nebulous flickerings, but within a week they'd intensified to a bright reality that pushed the solid universe into soft focus. Daniel began to swim, without option, in a fog of celestials. She was subject to a rare sensitivity, one that without warning would open her up to a past dimension, where she bore witness to titanic heavenly battles. And before long, the sight of swirling and gyrating armies of angels and demons were as much part of her day as a visit to the corner store.

Her parents were troubled by their daughter's propensity to freeze and glaze over, but assumed it to be no more than hormonal disruption, and said nothing. Renee, knowing her parents' need

Angels & Demons

for an ordered house, held back, and kept her altervisions to herself.

Unbeknownst to Daniel, the Celestial War she was viewing in all its clamoring magnitude, had not been fought between the forces of good and evil as earthly misconception would have it, but between two sides equally matched in their mixture of honor and malice. A conflict not of right versus wrong, but a territorial dispute emanating from the very elements that make Purgatory a permanent necessity— namely, unresolved internal conflicts.

When the Great War ended in treaty and the angels and demons realigned, there was no longer any strife, and the pact of separation made possible the oxymoronic pairings that became fundamental to the formation of the Purgatory Bureau.

Today the P.B.'s bipartisan agents continue to work in angel-demon duos, in a cooperative attempt to maintain Purgatory's state of harmony.

Daniel had been powerless to stop the sights of berserk angels and bloody demons, and by rights should have been filled with uncontrollable fear. But she wasn't. She accepted the happenings with a wide-eyed wonderment, safe in some inner knowledge that the visions would bring her no harm. When it

Badge of the
Second Airborne
Commissariat.

became clear that the fiery spirit world was destined to stay with her, she decided to hunt for proof of her sightings within the tangible world. Her findings were slim, an arrow head, a slither of shield, but they were enough to sustain her confidence in the empirical existence of her experiences.

The collection she assembled was amorphous, and to most eyes would have been no more than an irregular assortment of scraps. But Daniel instinctively understood that these remains were permeated with all the contradictions she would later face in Purgatory. Daniel had no religious faith or belief, nor did she see the relics as magical. Her collection was simply a magnification of realism, and she wanted it because it represented a truth she found nowhere else.

To Renee Daniel her arrival in Purgatory was in itself a vindication. Any lingering fears of her insanity were instantly dispelled. She found herself in her element, able to fully verify her visions and the spectacles that had dominated the majority of her life.

Here in the Museum, access to the P.B.'s historical files and relics allowed Daniel to put her own collection into context, and mount the comprehensive archive that constitutes her room.

Daniel was so delighted with her finds in Purgatory and particularly the P.B.'s archives, that it took her a considerable period before she was willing to assess her own position. When she eventually began confronting the dichotomy her split world had demanded of her, she was flabbergasted by her own resilience. The task of realigning herself was akin to that of the reunification undertaken by the celestials, and with that example in mind, she managed to forge a partnership that permitted her soul and its shadow to go forth into Avalon and Pandemonium respectively.

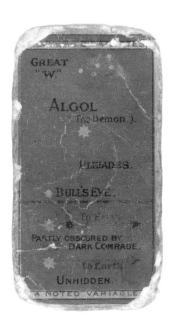

LEFT AND FAR LEFT:
Morningstar Algol
ticket outbound from
Orcus; Luciferian bill
of transit.

ABDIEL CHAMUEL JOPHIEL MICHAEL

ABOVE AND LEFT: *Bottled angel essence.*

RIGHT: *Broken snake arrow, discovered in Ireland by R. Daniel.*

FACING PAGE: *Archangel reincarnation hat.*

ZACHIEL

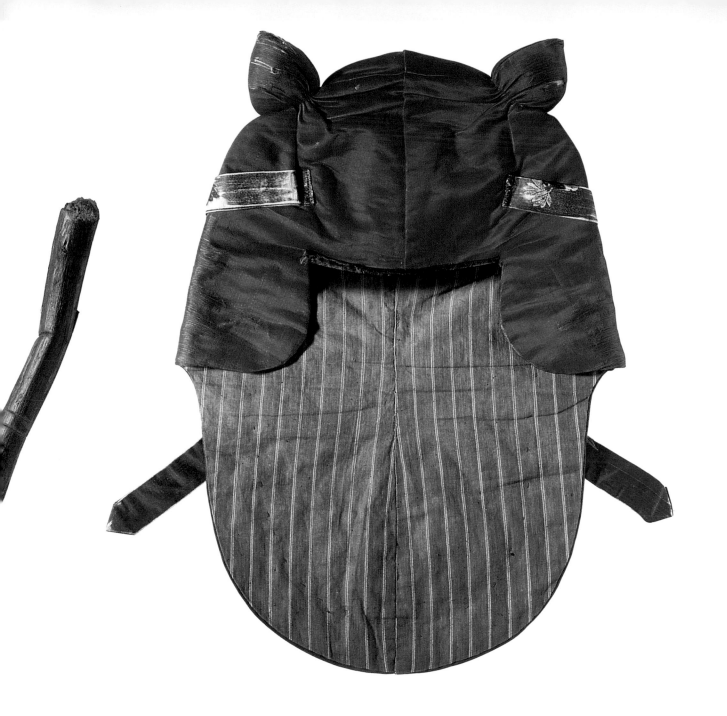

FACING PAGE: *Baron del Tere de Cardaillac St. Paul's sketchbook.*

FACING PAGE, INSET: *Celestial Certificate of office (25 Para), entitling Baron del Tere de Cardaillac St. Paul to enter the P.B. archives. The Baron was a man so determined to observe his past life in a sanctimonious light, that he found himself diligently recording the domain he'd been assiduously avoiding.*

THIS PAGE: *The Baron's portrait of a prominent daemon.*

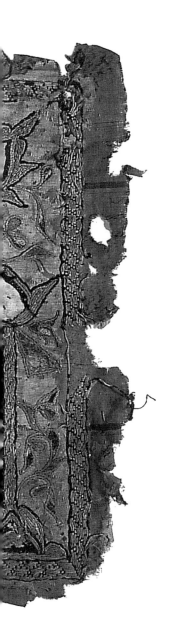

ABOVE: *Volatiles: four Angelica and a fugitive Djinnsing.*

LEFT: *Rakshasa hellion's wing-gill on its preservation shroud.*

RIGHT: *Sealed incubation dome containing root hobgoblin.*

PART TWO
The Curator's Tale

THE CURATOR'S TALE

I emerged into Purgatory's light via the stone steps that lead anti-clockwise around the inner wall of the Dreamwell. Although I'd been subliminally aware of a sensation of climbing and a growing babble of voices, I didn't come to full consciousness until I was about twenty feet from the stairhead.

There is always a noisy throng leaning on the huge circular balustrade overlooking the Dreamwell. Some go there to gaze at the great swirling mass of images generated within its center, others to watch the arrivals, seeking out familiar faces or just observing the newly dead passing through their transition from confusion to recognition.

I have since been told that by the time a newcomer reaches the low gateway at the head of the steps, he or she receives back their living memory, and are thus able to proceed with the task ahead of them.

When I reached the final step, I had not the slightest notion of who I might have been.

My disorientation must have been obvious, because a tall woman, in a tangerine summer dress, who was standing close by, inquired if I needed assistance. I stuttered somewhat stupidly, "Where am I?"

"You're in Purgatory," she responded. Then seeing my continued befuddlement, asked me my name and from which century I'd come. I replied that I had no idea. That seemed to surprise her, and after a second or two she suggested that I walk further down the street to get myself identified at the Bureau.

I followed her directions, and started off along the wide avenue bordered with Etruscan elms, trying frantically to make some sense of what was happening. Certainly I was dead, though I had no recollection of dying. Was I really in Purgatory; it didn't look like any Purgatory I'd ever heard of. But how could I possibly be aware of that—because if I had no memory, I would have no knowledge of any of the things I'd heard. I considered the problem, and concluded that for some peculiar reason my mind must have limited itself to retaining non-personal information.

By the time I reached the Bureau's fenced grounds, I had begun to convince myself that I was adjusting to my surroundings, when a casual glance back down the avenue made me jump. The huge elms were gone, and in their place stood a row of delicate plum maples. I shook my head in disbelief, turned back to the silver-gray granite Bureau building and got another shock. At first sight it had appeared daunting, but in those few seconds of distraction, its color had taken on a distinct purplish hue, it had grown a third turret on the roof and its countenance had become welcoming. Peculiarly enough, these alterations to my surroundings didn't unnerve me as much as I would have expected. But that didn't stop me from approaching the entrance with considerable caution, half expecting that the building would suddenly mutate into a white rabbit.

I eased through the narrow paneled double doors, and stepped into the entrance hall. A large semicircular desk stood at the hall's center and I strolled up to it with all the calm I could muster. Seated behind the desk, playing an ornate board game I didn't recognize, were a pair of individuals so physically different I could only gape. To my left squatted a massive luciferian creature with a fierce, leathery head and great black protruding eyes. Beside him sat perched a delicate, pale, ethereal figure, who inquired in a polite hoarse whisper whether *they* may be of some assistance.

Having no other way to describe my situation, I blurted out that I didn't know who I was, and had no idea why I was in Purgatory, and could they please tell me what I should do. The ethereal one fixed me with his translucent gray eyes and replied, "My friend, you're meant to do the same as everyone else here—assess the life you've just vacated. As for not knowing who you are, that is, I admit, a considerable handicap. It must be very uncomfortable for you, being a stranger to yourself."

I wanted to say, "Of course it bloody well is!" but instead, I kept my mouth shut and nodded my affirmation.

As if reading my mind, the demonic creature stared hard at me, and then in a sonorous and smoothly cultured tone it spoke, "Have you by any chance perused your person? It is possible that you're carrying something that might give clue to your identity?"

Oddly I hadn't thought of checking my clothing. I put my hands in my pockets and came out with two beautifully carved netsuke, one rabbit and one squirrel. I held them in my outstretched palms for the three of us to examine. In a sense the two tiny figures were deeply familiar to me, I knew them intimately, and yet I had no knowledge of how I got them or why I carried them. I started to try to explain this to the Bureau's agents but the angelic one held up his long white hand, smiled benevolently, and said, "I would hazard a guess that you're wanted at the Museum, I expect the curator's awaiting your arrival. Don't worry, these things sort themselves out." Then, as if to prohibit further questions, he gave me directions to the Museum, bowed, and returned to contemplating his game.

Back in the street my senses tried to attune themselves to another change in the surroundings. What had been a wide expanse of pavement was now a series of parallel paths separated by narrow strips of clipped bluegrass. But the pleasant quietness hadn't altered and it was a delight to hear no cars or trucks anywhere—in fact I could detect no mechanical sounds at all.

At this point I should explain that although everything around me seemed strange, it also felt absolutely right—as though I'd known the whole environment for an eternity. The people, whether in groups or on their own, had an air of purpose; the buildings seemed finely proportioned; and even the quality of light felt as though it made objects crisper, yet more integral. I was entranced, and if only I'd had my memory, I might have been pleased to be dead.

When I arrived at the Museum, Thomas Vey was waiting to receive me. I didn't know he was the curator, but by his affable and proprietorial manner I could tell he was someone of authority. He ushered me through the porchway and into the marble vestibule, taking my arm and telling me that he'd been warned to expect me. We passed through a number of rooms filled with all manner of artworks, before we entered into what I presumed to be his private office. He offered me one of the armchairs, and when I was seated, asked to see the netsuke. I passed them to him, and he examined them carefully, making appreciative grunting noises. Finally he looked up and said, "So you really have no idea who you are?"

"I'm afraid not," I replied.

"Nothing to be afraid of, dear boy. Mortal amnesia happens from time to time, rarely I admit, but it does happen. I think you'd better come and be with us for a while. We have no way of knowing whether you made or collected these two little animals. But either way all three of you are undoubtedly in need of sanctuary."

"Sanctuary?" I said, more defensively than I intended. "Why do I need sanctuary?"

"Because," he said "whether you're a collector or a creator, the Museum is going to be your best chance of finding out about your past. You could of course go into the city and wander around, on the off chance that you'll bump into someone who knew you. But even then, that's unlikely to solve the problem that's obstructing your memory. No, take it from me. This is where you should begin your search."

So I did as Thomas Vey suggested and submitted myself to his care and that of the institution he represented.

I worked each day in the Museum, under Curator Vey's supervision, learning how everything functioned and how to find my way around. Although quite small from the outside the Museum's interior is colossal: a warren of corridors, halls, and stairways leading to a virtually endless number of exhibiting rooms. The discrepancy between the outside and the inside was rather disturbing at first, but after the Mobius principle of expanding cubic capacity had been explained to me, I became passably comfortable with the structural unreliability of my new home.

At night I didn't sleep, but that wasn't unusual, as no one sleeps in Purgatory. There's no need to dream, therefore sleep is redundant. I required no bed or bedroom, and the size of the Museum ensured that if I wanted seclusion I could find a comfortable, out of the way spot to secrete myself. The library was my favorite perch, and it was there that I came across the writings of Fra Gabrielle, who developed a system of belief revolving around the notion of three belongings: belonging to oneself and the discovery of one's internal theater; belonging to the universe and the unification that comes with sensual bliss; and belonging to one's ancestry and the earth beneath one's feet. They're such simple graces, yet they evoked in me the disquieting certitude that I had failed abysmally on all three accounts.

When the daylight faded to darkness I would go out into the city and stroll the streets, parks, and thoroughfares. As I walked I tried to force myself into remembering, but as Curator Vey had predicted it was not within my power to so. After a few weeks I stopped trying to squeeze my memory and attempted to accept that my history would return to me when it was ready. The city intrigued me—its changing facade, its fluxing mass of multi-raced humanity all striving directly or indirectly to come to terms with themselves. Every aspect of earthly condition, apart from violence, seemed to be occurring within the city's boundaries. No harsh words were spoken, no cruelty was ever exhibited. And yet this wasn't a Utopia; the need to move on was present in all of us.

As time passed I grew even more familiar with the Museum. I spoke regularly with Curator Vey, sat in as observer on some of his consultations with the collectors when they discussed their works and their life conclusions. I also spoke to those contributors privately. I was content to learn. I enjoyed being attached to the Museum, but I was neither a contributor nor a minder, because I was not actively engaged in self-evaluation. I couldn't move on to another State, since I was an unknown quantity. I asked the curator if he had any idea why my memory hadn't returned. He replied that, in his own life time, he'd refused to face his soul's calling, and when it lost patience with his propensity for denial, it had withdrawn and left him totally rudderless. If the same scenario applied to me, he surmised, then some event of magnitude may well have shattered my core, and cast my broken parts outwardly into space.

I asked gloomily if this meant I was permanently lost.

"No, no," he replied. "Space is elliptic, and one or another of those laws of astrodynamics has it designed so that all elements traveling outwards will eventually meet again at the same point. Fortunately for you, that place is right here. You just have to keep your eyes and ears open and sooner or later you will be able to piece yourself together. Do you know about Osiris?" he asked. I shook my head. "Osiris," he said, with a certain glee in his voice, "was killed by his brother Set. Set then cut Osiris into fourteen pieces, and scattered the parts throughout the world.

But, as dissembled as Osiris was, his soul mate Isis found each of the pieces and brought them back together to make Osiris whole. Inspiring tale, in a left-sided sort of way, isn't it?"

It may have been to Curator Vey, but I felt like I'd just been drawn and quartered.

Some weeks after our conversation, I caught the first glimmer of my past. I'd discovered a section of the Museum I'd never been in before (it wasn't the first time the Museum's organic unfolding had sprung a surprise on me). In an area dedicated to wall hangings, I came upon The Fitzgerald Room and the carpets therein. A plaque next to the carpets was inscribed with lines from Khayyam's poems. I followed the instructions, read the verses aloud and was enchanted to see the carpets come to life. While watching their story, some dormant part of my brain was triggered, and I saw for a half a second my hands encased in translucent plastic gloves. It was definitely a moment from my past—nothing monumental, but it was a shock. I quickly turned and left the room, heading back to more comfortable ground. It wasn't the single memory that disturbed me, it was fear that the dam would burst and I'd be swept away in a flood of unbearable truths.

It took me the best part of a day to get my courage together and go back to the carpets and when I did I was disappointed. Although I'd read all of Fitzgerald's account, and again witnessed Basa's tale, I had no more memory flashes. However I did get a strange sense of empathy with Fitzgerald, a kind of *knowing* how he felt, as though I had experienced some similar sense of petrified loss.

I went to see Curator Vey, when he was next free, and told him of my experience. He seemed pleased, but a little distracted. Eventually he gave me his full attention and said that he had something important to tell me. He went on to say that he had at last completed his own contemplation, and that the reason he had originally been given the role of Curator was the inevitability of his lengthy stay in Purgatory. Now that he was moving on from the city he must pass over his position to another whose condition rendered extended occupation a certainty. He realized I hadn't had time to make myself fully conversant with the Museum, but he had chosen me as his successor because I fitted the requirements and I knew enough about the curator's role to take on the job. I protested vehemently, saying that I had none of his wisdom or knowledge and was not up to the task. But he would not be dissuaded. As he put it, it was simply a matter of learning as I went along. I was not required to give advice, all I had to do was take proper care of the displays and be a good listener.

And so I became Curator. As I had no name, I was obliged to invent one, and for want of a better alternative called myself Curator Non.

No one came to tell me what to do, and I reported to no one. I just followed Curator Vey's example and continued the Museum's traditions as they had been shown to me.

One of my chief responsibilities was to give ear to the stories told by the contributors, and assist them in understanding the relationship between their collections and their past lives. In this one area at least, not having my own life as a comparison proved a blessing, as I was able to be attentive and respond without fear of bias.

The connection, as I learned by degrees, between a person's collection and their life's actions was inexorable. If, as my predecessor had explained to me, dreams were the manner in which one recorded and passed on one's experiences, then collections were the method by which one took in encrypted information from the collective unconscious. A collection was not only the beloved objects of an individual's life but the means of accessing the Dreamwell's accumulated wisdom. Also, through its omissions, a collection will point to the unresolved conflicts that have still to be breached in order that an individual might progress.

The gradual discovery of who I was, began with A. S. Winter. While talking with Alice and helping her assemble her room of obscure objects, I started to recognize certain trace elements, behavior patterns, things that felt distinctly familiar. I began to get short bursts of very vivid memory, only lasting a second or two but enough to be certain that they were my history and not my imagination.

Each of these clipped events was associated by a sense of isolation very similar to those Alice was describing. When I touched the objects in her collections an intense feeling of loneliness welled up in me.

Again I expected sudden revelation, only to be left hanging. It wasn't until my first encounter with Eugene Delancet, and his postal assemblage, that I experienced another bout of memory. This time it arrived as a snippet, like a scene from a home movie: I was clinging to my mother's leg, it was solid and familiar and I didn't want to let it go, not even for a second. She dragged along for a while, with me attached like a limpet, and then in obvious exasperation reached down, pried my hands away, and smartly placed a closed door between us. I had been deserted, I was heartbroken and furious. True she had only gone to the bathroom, but it was without me, and the desolation cascaded over me in vast self-pitying waves. I vowed never to forgive her.

After that restored memory, I began to recognize the signs. I'd search out those contributors whose works and lives I responded to overtly. When I discovered a suitable individual I would make myself fully available to assist him or her, in order to tease out another of my memories.

The remembrances were different in type and nature of conflict. For example, in Otto Sengler's case, I was in the middle of reading his *Sfumatoglyphic* text when the following came back to me: before sleep one night, I was troubled by my lack of conviction. I asked myself how to overcome this weakness. I remember thinking as I dropped off, "I need to . . . I need to . . ." When I awoke I brought from a dream, the image of a row of frogs chorusing, "Rivet, rivet." The word wouldn't stop running through my head. I considered its literal meaning, but it held nothing of the quality I searched for. So I started juggling the letters, but could find no reasonable anagram. Then I said to myself these words are plural, they're RIVETS, and immediately the letters regrouped and I saw the completion to the previous night's sentence: "I need to . . . STRIVE." And strive I had, but for what?

From Gazio I learned of my romantic compulsion, from Levant a tendency toward ironic anarchy, and Amorfe made me realize I'd been an obsessive perfectionist. Cavarn's fear of the future I knew only too well, Nathius' extreme competitiveness was undoubtedly in my makeup and as for Renee Daniel, I too knew what it was like to see the world with a contradictory vision.

Curator Vey's prophecy appeared to be coming true. My life had been a seemingly never-ending stream of evasions and unaccepted ambivalence. Those fragments of myself cast into space were returning via the collectors I was collecting.

The information I had acquired about myself drew me closer to my goal, but I could sense I needed one further insight to unleash the full extent of my memory. I thought of the first flash I'd had in the Fitzgerald room and the kinship I'd felt with the carpets. I went back, and stood before the six eyes. They watched me and I waited. I held out against their penetrating glare, and then without warning my resistance crumbled, I sank to my knees and as I mumbled out their verses, the carpets showed me my life. And what I saw, and what I knew were one and the same.

My name was Sage Semeuse. I was a doctor, and I lived all of my life in Paris. I was married with two children, Jean and Dominique. I called Jean my squirrel and Dominique my rabbit. I had a passion for netsuke.

At 11.30 a.m. on the 22nd of June 1983, I was standing in my surgery looking through the window at the trees in the Luxembourg Gardens. I was pleasantly contemplating my lunch options, when the receptionist rang through to tell me that the last client of the morning had arrived. A few seconds later she ushered in a woman of medium height and weight, medium hair color and complexion, and even medium age. The moment I set eyes on Madame Gornier I knew what I wanted to do with her. It was such an arrogant thought that it should have been dismissed immediately, but because I let it linger, it took root and once established, would not leave me.

Doctoring, in my case, meant cosmetic surgery. I had dedicated my skills to changing people's appearances, sometimes for very good reasons, but mostly to appease their vanity and because they paid me exceptionally well. I'd become a very wealthy man, carving cartilage and grafting skin, and I'd grown used to my patients treating me with the exaggerated respect one gives a magician.

By rights, I should have been a very different kind of doctor. My father had offered to retire early and let me take over his general practice, but I had rebuffed him, saying I wished to continue my studies and become a surgeon. When I proved to be the best in my class, I was offered the chance to specialize in neurosurgery, but again I declined. I wanted creature comforts and knew exactly how to go about getting them. I also knew that I had been blessed with the ability to heal, and that my soul's course demanded I use my gift. But I stilled the voice of honest pursuit, choosing instead to feather my nest by peddling glamour.

When Marie Louise Gornier stepped into my office that June morning the notion that struck me was this: It is one thing to correct ugliness, another to enhance beauty, but to take a face and body and transform them from ordinary to magnificent, that would be a worthy feat.

I suppose I had grown bored or maybe my ego had inflated to the point where I felt that the gods guided my hands. Whatever the reason, I set about convincing Marie Louise that, far from simply ironing out the wrinkles around her eyes, we should begin a total refurbishment. Marie Louise, like many women who end up on my operating table had a gullible streak. Not to say she was stupid, far from it, she was simply insecure in a world that places heavy emphasis on first appearances, and she found it almost impossible not to be lured by my slick tongued temptations.

Surgery commenced two days later—I began with her face. That would take the most work and I was going to need a number of passes if I was to take my sculpture to the kind of finish I had in mind. I kept thinking about my favorite netsuke pieces and the exquisiteness of their detail. Obsessed with the idea of perfection, I subjected Marie Louise to my concepts of ideal beauty. Her nose, her eyes, her cheeks, her lips and even her ears, I remolded again and again until I was satisfied. Her body took less work. I removed a little fat on the legs and buttocks, added a little to her breasts—as for the rest, the repeated surgery had sapped her appetite, so her figure shrunk of its own accord into the current vogue.

I thought that when I was done with her I would feel proud of my handiwork. I half expected to be excited enough with the results to want to seduce her. But I didn't, instead I felt a deep disquiet. I look back now and see that my disgusted soul was making a last effort to make me acknowledge my appalling behavior. I'm not sure what I could have done to make recompense but at least I could have owned up to my excesses. In spite of this inner distaste at my manipulations, I put my arm around Marie Louise, told her the world was her oyster, and hurried her out of the door. When she was gone I forced myself to mentally file her away in the cabinet marked "success."

But Marie Louise was not a success, she was a disaster. The grafting didn't take properly, infection set in and her breasts tried to reject the implants. One month later, she returned to me looking truly terrible. I put her on a course of drugs to waylay the infection, but it seemed to make little difference. I increased the drug dosage and removed the implants. The sores on her face started to dry out, but her body was taking on water and her joints were swelling. I operated on her face again, trying to make good the damage, but I felt crude and my hands performed clumsily.

When the bandages came off, it was plainly obvious I'd made matters worse. Her face was even more of a mess. I was worried she would re-infect and I gave her an even stronger drug—her whole body started to swell. I became desperate, I should have asked for help, but I was too embarrassed. Things went from bad to worse and by the time she was hospitalized she looked like a plague victim.

It was no surprise to discover that I was being sued by Marie Louise's lawyers, for every centime I owned. In a way I felt almost relieved. I wanted to make amends, to admit that I'd dissected her like an insect, that I should never have operated, should never have become a plastic surgeon. A trial would have given me absolution, but the suit was settled out of court. I was bankrupt, my hands wouldn't stop shaking, and even if I could have taken up a scalpel again I would never have been able to score flesh with it.

I crumbled quickly from that point. My wife (who had always been more interested in my earning powers than my health and happiness) left me, taking the children with her. And in less than two years I was dead—beaten to death by a drunk outside a lingerie shop on Rue Fontaine. I was aged 53 years, four months and three days.

It's taken me a long while to get over the impact of who I'd been, and for that matter, who I still was. Denial was futile but I tried anyway. I could admit that the crimes against Marie Louise were crimes against humanity, but I could not accept that the moronic predictability of my behavior had rendered me a failure in the eyes of the collective unconscious.

I have kept the name Curator Non, partly because it remains apposite and partly because I feel anything but Sage-like.

There's still much to be sifted through before I'm able to leave Purgatory, but I've begun assembling the Non Room. And I'm pleased to say that little by little the netsuke find their way to me.

With memory comes a loss of innocence, and lately I've found skepticism creeping in. Do I truly understand my position here in Purgatory? Can I trust anything I've written in this thesis of redemption? Or am I an unborn, tricked into the position of eternal civil servant to an ethereal bureaucracy that neither cares for, nor considers, the pathetic individuals trapped within its eternal arcane web? Can we trust that there are any postmortal certitudes? Why do I persist in imagining the Dreamwell to be a celestial apothecary, when in fact it's probably no more than a purveyor of sadistic jokes and cruelly complex farces? Is this all just a never-ending fall from grace? These thoughts, and many others, eat away at me. But then I remind myself that a true skeptic suspends his judgment, holding off the morbid doubts as fervently as he does the craving for a benevolent universe. My mind is by definition less reliable than my senses and as I can smell, see and hear Purgatory in all its subtly changing integrity, I choose to believe that my deadlock will be resolved and that eventually I will pass beyond this city to a new State.

It would seem to me that in death, unlike life, we no longer suffer from the socially enforced collusion that requires us to accept a single version of reality. Here, at this mid point, each of us dismantles our past and builds anew our own view of existence.

WITHOUT END

.